fever

Gerry Feehily was born in London and grew up in Ireland. After his studies he lived in Japan, Italy, and Spain before settling in Paris. His articles on French literature and European politics have appeared in the *Independent*, *New Statesman*, and the *Irish Examiner*. He is currently working on *The Inner Circle*, his second novel.

fever

Gerry Feehily

PARTHIAN

Parthian
The Old Surgery
Napier Street
Cardigan
SA43 1ED

www.parthianbooks.co.uk

First published in 2007
© Gerry Feehily 2007
All Rights Reserved

ISBN 978-1-905762-35-4

Editor: Jasmine Donahaye

Cover design by Marc Jennings
Typeset by Lucy Llewellyn
Printed and bound by Dinefwr Press, Llandybïe

The publisher acknowledges the financial support of the
Welsh Books Council.

British Library Cataloguing in Publication Data

A cataloguing record for this book is available from the
British Library.

For Mai and Hugh

A very small degree of hope is sufficient
to cause the birth of love.
Stendhal

From how many crimes, wars, murders, calamities, cruelties
would mankind have been delivered had some man then
uprooted the fences and filled up the ditches.
Count Lev Tolstoy

Oh God bless England is our prayer!
Whack for the diddle of the die do day!
Irish folk song

Part One

1.

I know about love, somehow.

So I started carrying rubbers on me.

It was the women from the North, from Belfast and Derry, the cities, and agreement is universal as to what this meant:

a) either they were gone on religion big time

b) else they gave themselves gladly to love

c) sometimes it was both.

I was beginning to get tuned in. I picked stuff up from songs, the odd poem, the movies.

Though as to what I knew of life I shall leave some suspension points thus...

I could have swung off a golden chandelier like Errol Flynn if there'd been any, but all the grand Prod houses had been knocked down.

I

Bungalows stood in their place. Bungalows and wind.

There was an ancient number a black woman sang – you give me fever, she said.

Though I hadn't seen the video I could tell by her voice that she knew what she was on about.

You give me fever.

She got me thinking about William Shakespeare somehow: the bit where Lear is holding Cordelia in his arms, Cordelia being dead at this moment, and he says her voice was ever soft, gentle and low, an excellent thing in woman.

That was how the black woman sang. Gentle and low.

Brothers and sisters of Atlantic bungalows, Atlantic wind, I know about love.

It's a fever.

It was McHugh who had a box of rubbers, him having experience in this and other such matters. I was up in his house when he leaned over and said, Look into my eyes and be well advised.

I took a look at them and said, You been smoking quare stuff.

Not, he replied, this is a different shade of haggard, if you dig.

I thought about it a second. Jammy man jammy, I said.

He told me he'd been running up stairs and pirouetting down corridors till about five o'clock that morning after a naked woman called Bernie who'd got a skull tattoo on her left buttock. From Ballygalley, up North, and renting one of the flats across the street that his folks owned. That night, as Ballygalley Bernie tossed her knickers at a lampshade and spun her bra out the window and laughed her head off, her husband in ground control one floor below slept in his Ireland shirt, blind drunk, his mouth open, the pillow dribble dark.

He snores, the brute, she said, showing McHugh the blue marks she got for not loving him enough.

Then they smoked a tenspot of Red Leb, and she said, If you don't look, you could think there was something prehistoric in the room, like an animal bumping into the furniture.

No, I couldn't say I was jealous of my friend El Señor Finbar McHugh – my mind was on higher stuff, this being the second day of my attack on Western Europe, after all.

I mustered my Red armies on the German, Italian and Spanish borders, grabbed the dice and rubbed them full of a mighty will, so as to restore peace, *fraternité* and all round good vibes to the troubled continent, but somehow I was reminded that only the night before Esmerelda Murphy had pulled him off in the jacks of Planet 2001, so I gave the table a kick and it all blurted out –

So have you some rubbers left or what, Mister Nocturnal Emissions? I said.

Keep it down, brother, said McHugh.

We listened out for the tightened buzz of parental presence behind the door, homing in on accounts of this our mid-summer bacchanal, but it was just Atlantic wind that rattled the doors. Dundrug's own.

Though as folks went Ma and Pa McHugh kept it discreet most times. Not only did they see out the day three floors down but they slept there too, leaving McHugh half a dozen chambers like a Regency buck. He didn't say why. He wondered if I preferred they spy on us, like normal parents.

I thought it strange nevertheless. But his was a Northerner blow-in family – his folks having come over from Belfast back in the seventies when it used to be all splattery hot there, when, if you crossed the wrong man you could end up not breathing for

3

ever. So they were low key on the communication front. Or at least there was a centre of low keyness – Pa McHugh.

Finbar the son was a lighter shade of dour. Must've used up half a box this week, he said. There's this latex waft all about me, like!

He tendered his fingers across the table. I was supposed to smell but I lurched out of my chair and headed for the window, through which spider-leg titanium towers loomed, and spacepods zipped along the air highways of our year of grace 4001.

Actually it was but a great plain of twentieth-century Atlantic ocean out there, just a section of Tievebawn mountain, with IRA – a bit grassed over now – painted in giant letters up on the summit, to welcome intruders.

Welcome to the Real.

Below me, citizens in summer wear, strictly non-climate adapted, were working against the blasts of Atlantic air towards Dundrug Central for evening mass.

+ Pray for us Sinners +

Never mind, for we worshipped other gods. Cos the McHughs had this ancient music centre and an older brother who'd entrusted Finbar with a collection of 33 rpm vinyls. For instance, there was that album Bowie did in Berlin with electronic blurps coming out of one speaker and Japanese guitar dootling from the other, recorded when he and Iggy Pop were teeth-grinding coke-snorters strung out by the Wall.

Far-travelled McHugh swore that Berlin was the most depressed city in the world Wall or Not and that Bowie looked like a fucking bender, and his missus, the stunning black one, was a lad dressed up, so most of the time we compromised with Led Zep 4 which was all about sylvan groves, ethereal women and all that posh shite English art student boys go in for.

4

But now we had on television – Marquee Moon!

I sat down again. Keep yer testicular happenings to yerself, I said, and go on and give us two rubbers.

I picked the dice up. Otherwise, I said, you might have to keep me company at my shotgun wedding.

I flung the dice across the board. I was supposed to be invading Rule Britannia next, but I just got three ones.

McHugh picked up the dice and blew onto them, and then I realised I'd left my backside exposed around by the Bering Strait.

Kamchatka, thou milk-livered Z, he intoned, and I reckoned he'd blown some Alex of Macedonia luck onto his dice, cos he threw the number of the Beast, three sixes.

The scene turned into one of ultra slaughter.

Yes, we were low-tech types. Our peers might have been coated in sweat as their brains went back a billion years over the latest Nintendo but we, understand, specialised in Risk, the board game of world domination, were Clausewitz disciples, sent out armies across the continents, knew the wrench when we saw a regiment wiped out.

Okay, they might have been bits of coloured plastic and all, but still. Me, I always went for Red cos I specialised in the CCCP, history-wise, and I wondered what Leon Trotsky and Vlad Ilyich would have made of this town if I'd hired them out as revolutionary consultants.

Out of badness McHugh chose the blue. Like an accountant he said he preferred the constitutional road to progress.

That's if he didn't go with green, like now. For Ireland!

He put the dice down and said, Do you want the ribbed or cherry-flavoured ones?

Just give us those you haven't used, I said.

I picked up the dice and started my defence of Mother

5

Russia, which, owing to the way the map was cut up, was strictly for yer banzai kamikazes.

McHugh said, Just one, so. Sure you haven't even lost your maidenhood, like.

I chose to ignore such a dig and concentrated on coveting his wallet, him being the only sixteen-year-old buck in Dundrug's jetset (membership – 2) who needed one, a burgundy leather number picked up in Majorca. He pulled it out of his back pocket and flipped it open. Like the man was loaded, loaded. He had a wedge of tens in there with the baldy scholastic monk of the shifty eyes, and a flush of twenties depicting our great national gasbag – WB Yeats.

Oh children of Eire, and me bollocks on fire etc

I never knew where he got the money. It wasn't politic to ask, cos sometimes he hung with the Dundrug Hard Brigade, which occasionally had a hand in the odd break in. He handed me one rubber and I said, Are you seeing Ballygalley Bernie tonight?

I don't know, he said, counting his remaining ones. She reckons the husband might be entertaining some doubts. Plus, she says she loves him deep down.

He stood up and gazed at the board. Anyway, I have other dark intentions, he said. Staggering in their deviousness, piping hot as my trews.

Ominous, I said.

He looked at the Risk board. Then he crouched, punched the air, first left, then right, Kung Fu-style.

The world is Ireland's, he said.

I slipped into my parka coat with the secret pocket – an old sock I'd sewn into the lining.

Not if I can help it! I said.

The blood of our Fenian dead, he said, in the Siberian snows.

We turned out of the living room and tripped down the stairs three two one. Chez McHugh was, by Dundrug standards, three storeys of ampleness, most houses in these parts being pebble-dash bungalows based on real dwarves' measurements.

Back in the seventies when most of the town was but a skitter of cottages between the coast and Tievebawn, Old Man McHugh got the place off some Prods for a couple of pounds and a cup of tea.

I gave the chandelier in the hallway a push, waved Howya, class woman! at the painting of a Prod ancestor in a ball gown with broad shoulders white like church marble.

Then we were inside The Chemist.

It was what everyone called the shop Ma and Pa McHugh ran on the ground floor. I don't know why. It must have been the same as the Railway Lounge, the Presbyterian Church, the Lighthouse. Back in the middle ages, a Chemist had stood there. The aeons passed, empires fell, kings were born, and the name stuck.

At The Chemist you could get newspapers, Curly Wurlies, fags, a dusty bottle of Wilkins Mulled Wine for that Christmas lift. But regarding antibios or tablets you went to see Bridget Doyle up Main Street.

She's got everythin' ye need, said Ma McHugh, when German tourists walked in.

Business looked slow. Nevertheless, McHugh's folks had a brand new Merc, which led me to surmise that maybe once upon a time, when he hadn't yet taken up watching TV twenty-four-seven that is, McHugh's old man used do a run across the border before it was Peace over there, and the bog sucking Irish Republic got rich on ten per cent annual growth, whatever that means.

7

I reckoned he used to deal in Embassy Regals, or maybe even rubbers when the Irish Free State in its wisdom didn't distribute them, sold them to the Northerners when their own supplies ran out.

We slipped into the backroom behind the shop. Pa McHugh was sitting with the light off in a photon bath of Ulster Television.

Anything good on, Mister McHugh? I said.

He kept on looking at the TV through the tinted specs which coped with the world for him.

Oh it's yourself, Jerome, he said.

McHugh Junior hurumphed. Actually, it's his special clone, he said.

I forked my fingers and crossed my arms over my chest like the leader of some planet who was curious about Planet Earth's strange addiction to glowing boxes with pictures inside them.

Ah now, said Pa McHugh, taking off those big double-glazed windows and all of a sudden his eyes were like a mole's, underground creases, if that's possible.

He rubbed the specs off of a hanky and put them back on – the eyes were re-established – ie globular and evasive, looking past yer head as though the patterns on the wallpaper contained reminders about things he'd forgotten.

Go easy in the town tonight, it's stirring up, he said.

How would you know? said McHugh.

Been living here a while.

Then like a mole he slipped back into his silence, just the TV twittering along, gloops of primary colour splashing his glasses.

McHugh rolled his eyes.

We pushed through the red yellow blue plastic streamers separating us from the shop, where Ma McHugh was looking

8

out the window onto the street. She sparked up a fag off her gold lighter, and a blue halo rose above her like a message from the gods.

She always smoked Rothmans Extra King Size, these mega-long fags with a gold band about the filter that suggested you had higher aspirations, like porcelain baths and knickers from Paris or something.

I didn't smoke myself, but if you went for a native brand like stubby wee Majors, for instance, your aspirations sort of tended towards becoming a farmer or something.

You boys hitting town? she said, looking out the window.

Mass, said McHugh.

Mass my bum, youse are going up town.

I swear we're going to Mass, Ma, said McHugh.

She turned away from the window. Ma McHugh was this tall spring-stepped Swedish looking beauty with a hearty laugh and big into golf. She wore cream satin blouses, black cotton slacks, and bangles rattled off her wrist. There was always this goldy silvery vibe about her hair which sat stiff like a saucepan on her head and wherever she went she was accompanied by frisks of perfume.

Like yer spikes, son, she said, stretching out her hand and touching my head. Very cosmopolitan.

In a cloud of smoke, she went behind the counter, her hips going left and right and back. Got a present for you, she said.

Oh no, I muttered.

For Ma McHugh also went to Lourdes once a year, had been up a stretch of Croagh Patrick on her knees, and I regretted ever having told her I'd given up on God.

I guess I upped the stakes the day I struck a Jesus pose at her, saying, Blessed are the spaceships, menataw, menetaw, ram, ram, like I was breaking into the devil's tongue.

9

She'd told me it all went back to when she was Bubbles McLoughlin – a hostess for British Airways on the Belfast-London run. A few minutes after take off everyone started screaming cos an engine just fell off the wing and plumped into the Irish sea and she promised God that if he spared her life she'd never drink again.

And He listened, she said. And I lost the Bubbles nickname.

Which must be why she had that crinkly-eyed Life is Good and People are So Interesting bounce about her which verged on scary.

She rooted through a drawer, picking out a Lourdes Virgin Mary swishing with holy water plus some mass cards of defunct McHughs and McLoughlins. She handed me a hologram of Padre Pio.

Padre Pio, the Italian mystic, with a beard in the form of a shovel, these wrathful brown eyes, and big crusty stigmata. Faced with the see-through holes in his hands, I lacked the Herr Doktor Freud lingo to describe his condition.

Aye, well, picking at them scabs he was, hi, I said.

You're doomed you pagan but sure go ahead and keep it, she said. Kid from Dunfagart with a lump in the brain prayed to the same one, and the lump's gone. Might do you some good.

Might get rid of the lump in his pants, said McHugh.

What's that, Finbar?

The lump between his shoulders. His head.

I slipped the mass card into my pocket, and, despite my godlessness, it didn't burn a hole in it. Didn't matter what she said, I always went along with her, just hoping she wasn't going to go into the Third Secret of Fatima, a few scraps of which some bishop from Fermanagh had let her in on. Stuff such as black-eyed bambinos seeing the divine mother, getting the low-down on Armageddon, the gnashing of skulls or whatever brought out this residual caveman side of me that believed it.

Ma McHugh gave her son a push and then slipped a twenty into his pocket. Who's winning the Risk, by the by? she said.

Pontius Pilate here, said McHugh, indicating me with his thumb.

The mother pulled on her Rothmans.

Don't know much about war, me, but beware of women plucking fluff from yer shirts, she said, as we made to go.

Why that? I said, turning.

It's what animals do. It means ye are in!

She winked. Blue clouds furled and streamed like a weather map of a tropical gale about her.

Go away and break some hearts, she said.

2.

One thing I've neglected to mention up to now, oh my *compañeros y compañeras* in Socialism (death to traitors!) and it's that Dundrug has a cosmopolitan edge; not yer edge that shaves parmesan into a dainty balsamico dressing, mind – it was sort of blunt, but not too much, cos back in the nineteenth century, regional Prods used to come in bustles and parasols and top hats to take of the Atlantic air during the summer.

All two weeks of it, I mean.

It was that wee dab of worldliness that turned Dundrug into a tourist resort when Ireland was independent, the red post boxes got painted green and we didn't win in World War 2 (us being the one nation on Earth that's proud we didn't help defeat the Nazis, like).

It infused us with a character distinct from the hill-dwelling tribes of Dunfagart, Blasnagall, and Koonlagh, where they mixed PCP into cattle feed, so men grew tits, and as a result listened to AC/DC and other brain-damage fare.

For come July, Dundrug, when fully operational, boasted –

30 pubs, three of which had chairs and tables screwed into the floor.

5 amusement arcades. Lose yer money and fuck off.

4 fish and chip shops, outside of which late at night you could meet –

The Dundrug Brigade – local hospitality, headbutt style.

A fairground the star of whom was Handsome Mickey, AKA the Donkey Flattener, the fattest man for fifty miles.

3 nightclubs. Not for the faint-hearted!

And of recent times:

1 refugee centre, with friends from Afghanistan, Democratic Republic of Congo, and yer other war-torn faves.

Okay, I give up. We weren't that suave at all.

So whether you were on for throwing up between moonlit caravans, getting a smack in the gob, blowing away your dole money on the slot machines all on the same night...

...Dundrug was the place!

And the day in question was July 12th. Over the border in Craigavon or Lisburn the *übermensch* of Ulster were celebrating that time way back when they tamed the Gaels at the Boyne river. A jolly old rout back in sixteen-oh-something, but they've been harping on about it ever since.

I had nothing against them, but whenever I saw them gawns on telly, with their bowler hats, orange sashes and old-style shoes clumping down country lanes, I'd mutter, Lads, it's all over, we stopped the medication.

Never mind, for while they lit their bonfires, our nationalist brethren headed for the border and crossed into the People's Republic of Dundrugistan for the coming week, and fifty per cent of these refugees were female, precocious, urban.

Northern Ireland maidens = mayhem!

So McHugh and I were heading for the Love Fest along a seafront street from Victorian times imaginatively dubbed Bayview Road, each Victorian-style house boasting a front lawn out of which poked a stunted palm tree attaining a majestic four-foot-nothing in height and signposts declaring Casa Mia, Bella Vista and Rooms En Suite.

For some reason Dundrug, also known as the Las Vegas of the Republic, was big into Mediterranean words and plants which just never managed to relieve the sense that, Oh no, we're still in Ireland.

Example – grey Atlantic clouds were moving south in a vast herd like migrating Zebu and occasionally you got a spit in the face – rain.

However, swallows snipped and skitted through the air, and that buzz in the distance, the buzz of Main Street, Dundrug, had, for just this little July window, to pass for all the longing in the world.

McHugh, I said, I'm sorry to tell you this, but your Ma is kind of racy.

He said, That's kind of horrifying, Oedipus-wise, but fine.

I kicked a can in front of me. Give us one more rubber, right, I said.

So you can do my Ma?

Naw, just need one to practise with!

Go buy some yourself.

Aye, let Bridget Doyle my Ma's bowling partner know I need

a case of Durex please and one for yerself.

There's machines in the jacks at Mullen's.

Someone beat it up last week did you not see, I said, blushing.

We crossed the Bridge. At the end of it Punch Gilbride, Teabags Malone and Mustapha Moran of the Dundrug Brigade were huddled by the tourist office. With their hands in their pockets and standing at right angles to one another in a kind of bitter silence punctuated by the odd expletive, they looked like a Greek chorus that'd lost its lines.

Move on, the Second Coming's cancelled, boys, said McHugh, while he high fived them.

As usual I nodded at them and hung back.

Any of you bucks got a Zippo? said Punch with his long head like an exclamation mark.

For what? said McHugh.

Punch pointed at the EU flags hanging up over the tourist office roof.

Cop the Union Jack flying up there. When was the last time that happened?

1921, I muttered.

Mustapha Moran said, You'd know, you being an English cunt and all.

McHugh said, What's wrong with yer own lighter?

Wind, said Punch. It's too fast. Flame don't catch.

Story of your life, Punch.

Mustapha Moran started walking round me. What's with the hair? You look like a hedgehog on stilts, he said.

Just kind of expressing myself.

Never think of expressing yerself with a comb?

I'd rather cut off my foot, Francis.

Aye, well that just might happen.

14

We left them, headed for Dundrug's Golden Mile, which was about two hundred yards long.

McHugh said, Careful, Mustapha Moran's on yer case.

I felt something cold go down my back, like someone emptying a pint over it. About what, I said.

Remember back in National School when he used to come in late and you'd laugh cos he'd say, I forgot me socks?

When I'd just got over from London?

Aye, well, I think it traumatised him a bit.

I was taking in this new security threat as we passed a group of girls in black dresses, one of whom bumped into McHugh accidentally on purpose.

Really sorry, friend, she said, staring into his eyes really deep and haunted-like.

Good evening, he said, and moved on just as his mobile – such timing! – started bleeping.

He was on the phone selling his Dow Jones Futures or something when we hit Main Street, passing Mullen's amusement arcade and Fallon's chip shop with Northerners in football shirts piling in.

Like some blushing bride I virtuously lowered my eyes so as to avoid the blue gaze of a couple of lads wearing Celtic shirts sitting on the bonnet of a Ford Fiesta. One of them said, Where's your handbag, before tossing an empty can of Harp my way.

Oh children of Eire – what need ye of Nintendo when Friday night on Main Street is a hyper-real assault course known as Male Virility Rituals? Instructions: in Round 1 dodge the Jumping Jocks put off by the sight of spikes growing out the top of yer existence.

Otherwise lose your teeth!

But with arms as slim as a ballerina's, I was not the fighting kind, so I chose only to mutter You Fools! out of the side of my mouth, and then took the security option, while we drifted past Frankie Dwyer's Provo pub, to stay close to the kerb and avoid a stag party as it came stumbling out the doors decked in tricolours. Like a multi-legged beast it zigged and zagged along as though to compensate for the Earth's spin through outer space. Then the groom in a white wedding dress went Timber! and fell sideways onto the footpath, spreading his arms out like a horizontal Christ the Redemptor, Rio.

I see the light, he yelled, waving at the clouds and those odd shreds of blue which constituted the sky.

By now I'd made it intact to the BBQ Café, so afore the stag lads could entertain themselves at my expense, there was another catastrophe unfolding, as a man with a blond moustache and wearing a Brazil shirt which said Ronaldo on the back dropped to his knees and cried out, Leslie Leslie.

The stag party members pulled up in front of him and nudged each other.

Leslie Leslie, he screamed.

On the count of three, the stag party lads went hopping and skipping about the broken-hearted man singing, Here we go, here we go.

Leslie, Leslie, he yelled, as though the name were pain itself. McHugh nubbed his phone off, and said, Action.

Sitting on a window ledge was a girl with kinked black hair and brown eyes that were directed our way.

I felt my heart contract a wee bit. Cos in the midst of all this Irish wildlife, she was something like elegance.

Hallo stranger, she said.

Her voice was kind of low, underlined by that Northern Irish habit of sultrily terminating yer sentences with an interrogative up turn?

An excellent thing in woman, as Papa Lear might have it.

McHugh put his hands in his pockets. So you're here, he said.

Naw, just walking the hologram, like.

He sat down beside her, plucking this chemical-smelling Marlboro she was smoking from between her beringed fingers.

What's doing? he goes.

Hotel let me off tonight. I'm free!

He's been bawling his head off all this time, she added, taking the cigarette back from McHugh.

He's in love, I put in.

Aye, she replied, giving me a scan up and down which must have calculated the cool factor of my threads and face and maybe even a career prospect synthesis in the trillionth of a second. Who are you anyway?

Jerome, I said, shrugging because I knew I couldn't change certain things, like my name.

Jerome used to be English, added McHugh.

What's that got to do with the Bishop of Newry? she said.

McHugh shrugged. Dunno, just adds a dimension to his personality.

Well, Jerome, she said. You sound like a man who knows what he's talking about.

She pulled on the cigarette, the smoke fluming through her nose and mouth intermittently.

Wait till I tell youse, she said. I was down on the beach watching the surfers when a guy from Africa called Amadou, just out of the refugee centre, sits down beside me. And do you know what he said?

I don't.

He said the Irish landscape was beautiful and its people very hospitable.

She covered her face with her hands.

I'm so embarrassed, she said, but her eyes peeping out from between her fingers glittered.

How come?

Cos I laughed at him, is how. I said, You're welcome!

McHugh stood up. We're off so, he said.

She put some hair into her mouth, took it out again and said, Either of you gents see my wee sister?

I didn't even know she had a sister. What does she look like? I asked.

Like me, she said, widening her eyes. Uncanny. You been in Ireland long?

Six hundred years.

Don't I just know, she said, looking up at heaven, which was sort of obstructed by strato cumulus at that moment.

And I felt this wee thin filament pass between us, like a white crackle of current lighting up a cloud.

But I just waved at her.

Keep your eyes open, she cried, with a London accent, and be well.

Both of us walked into the amusement arcade.

Is that the one with the tattooed arse? I said.

That's another, that's Siobhan, said McHugh. Skull arse woman just phoned to say the husband found out. He burst into tears and promised to be good to her.

All's well that ends well so. So does yer one back there suffer from any specific illness?

McHugh was sorting through his change but now he jerked a little with surprise. Who you talking of?

18

A particularly violent strain of halitosis or something?

That one? If you fancy chatting to her, don't go bugging me, bug her.

He shrugged. I don't know, he added. She's complicated, like. Do you fancy her?

It's like certain symptoms are kicking in.

A kind of warm, melty ache in your guts?

Aye, something like to that.

Might be love, might be the skitters, who can tell.

We went down the main corridor, slot machines left and right going off. Everywhere the wrench of handles, the triple thunk as the spinning bars came to a stop, and here and there the odd sputter and chink of jackpot money hitting the trays.

It was like a nineteenth-century factory. The same principle, like. You pulled the handles and the machines always won.

Dundrug's intelligentsia (membership – 2) however, went for the poker machines, with their illusion of interactivity, and since my favourite machine just happened to be free, the one which seemed to be nicest to me despite the fact that even the lowest reptile was hotter on the sentiments front, I was starting to feel the gambler's tingle which said Fortune Smiles for Thee. I slipped a couple of fifty pence bits into the slot. Bet two credits a go. My first hand was three kings. A win. Then it was the double or quits moment.

A two came up. Beautiful. I slapped the high. Up came a King!

I press low to get an ace. Easy. Slapped Lo, and it was a Jack!

The Hi Lo buttons was flashing at top speed, and out of the speakers came a two-tone buzz HI LO HI LO HI LO designed to shatter your nerves and pump up the adrenalin.

My forehead was covered in sweat.

Them Jacks are bastards, said McHugh. Bet you'll get a Queen.

I covered my eyes and smacked the low button.

I heard the blip blip sounds of four hundred credits coming my way. I opened my eyes – a ten!

McHugh turned back to his machine and fed it more coins.

Machines must be in good form tonight, man, he said. Catch them while they is hot!

Just as I got two pair my Da came up behind and nudged me.

What's all this, he said, slipping a handful of fifty pence pieces into my pocket.

I'm up to thirty quid, I said. You busy tonight?

Da fiddled with his master keys and gave McHugh a dunt. Busy in Bedlam. You know them machines are programmed to pay out ninety percent?

That's a lot, said McHugh.

Never enough, said my Da, holding up his hands, which had a permanent green tinge due to all the coppers passing though them. A man out there in the street is just after losing a thousand pounds, he said. Thought he had a relationship going. With a computer.

Dark pagan beliefs, Mister Maguire, said McHugh.

Had to threaten the guards on him cos he wanted to beat it up.

Gambling leads to the unrighteous path.

You know any righteous ones?

In Dominus Ominus, said McHugh, crossing himself.

My old man scooted off.

Your Da's some gas man, said McHugh recovering from the blush which'd come over him, and I wondered what it were about, unless he reckoned my Da's powers extended to gazing into our blackened souls.

McHugh coughed, emptied more fifty pence bits into the

poker slot and proceeded to blow away a four of a kind.

After giving the machine a kick he said, She writes poetry.

Instinctively, I patted my poem notebook in my back pocket and my knee began to judder up and down in sympathetic vibration.

But I had to play it cool. What sort? I said.

She slipped me this poem once. And it was something about animals. Cavorting wild beasts. The fetid jungle.

Was it in rhymes and stuff?

I don't remember. All I know is that I didn't understand it. So it was like poetry.

Suddenly there was a girl right beside him wearing an old Wham teeshirt which said Choose Life and saying her friend fancied him.

That girl over there, she said, fancies you like mad.

Me and McHugh looked behind and this girl standing in a gap between two slot machines called Lucky Strike suddenly disappeared.

Her friend tittered.

Watching this man play poker, said McHugh.

Like you don't want to talk to her?

I'm re-evaluating my whole approach to sex, like.

Continue wee man, she said, and buzzed off.

Pause button, I said, girl with the Choose Life teeshirt she look okay.

If you even touched girl with Choose Life you'd probably get arrested for underage sex. She's probably a cop even.

Anyway, he said, slapping the machine, I'd have preferred her if her teeshirt'd said Fuck Life.

Describe your sombre thoughts, McHugh, I said.

They're in Brazil, on Ipanema beach where a crinkle-haired

metisse woman caresses me and she's not even a transvestite, like!

Aye, cos your local woman supply is just dried up, i'nt it?

Irish women kill me, man.

He stubbed his cigarette out on the floor. They know you too well. They try to get into your head.

That's a really tragic destiny, I said. Let's find yer woman.

Reluctantly I cashed in the twenty pounds I'd got left, though I would've preferred to jack them back up to thirty, but when we got back into the street McHugh's mobile was diddling away again and Siobhan had been replaced by Dominic the Merry who, as usual, was snickering to himself with his flies undone and his lad hanging out like an off-purple slug as scantily-clad girls cringed past him.

Mad as a duck, surviving on a diet of winkles and spuds, there were still about sixty per cent of people voting age in town who thought that when he used to fish Dominic'd found a bushel of gold sovereigns out in the bay, cos way back a galleon from the Armada had gone down there.

So it was said the sight of the Spanish skeletons had driven him mad.

Do it with suet! he yelled, and stood up with his unfortunate lad flopping about.

I watched as McHugh, on the phone to his L.A. agent or something, headed up the back lane of the amusement arcade. I checked my secret pocket and crossed the street, heading for Barry Gillan's Top Sounds shop.

To commit a crime!

There was a speaker hanging half nailed above the front door and you could hear dribbling out of it our international star PJ Burren singing My Darling of Dundrug.

When I was a cub, PJ was in his teens up the front of the

school bus, and the big smoking lads at the back used to creep up behind him and slap him on the head and slip stink bombs into his satchel, saying, Go on PJ, sing us a few bars!

He who laughs loudest, as they say, for once he left school, PJ started peddling his singles on the pilgrimage tours going to Knock. The next thing he was mega.

One hundred thousand grannies couldn't be wrong.

But somehow the music gnawed into my head and I just went into a trance on Main Street, Dundrug, as PJ sang –

> *My Darling of Dundrug*
> *I'd love to have a slug*
> *Of a Darling cup of Tea*
> *That you will brew for me*
> *We'll get married on the strand*
> *And I will hold yer hand...*

...and going past me was a nun, skirt whipping in the wind and eating a 99, a pair of Derry girls scratching along the footpath in six inch heels and Dance with my Sister I'm Sweating hats on their heads, and I was scanning to see if She was around.

This, I said to myself, is my summer of love.

Cheer up, I heard, it might never happen!

I surfaced, and it was Mustapha Moran in front of me. I felt my heart go in out like when you blow and suck into a crisp bag I was that scared. But just like a mafia hitman about to bump someone off, he bid me, all *tutti amici*, to sit with him on the bonnet of a Toyota Carola, and when he turned I saw there was DRUIDS written on the back of his jacket in Tippex.

Cigarette?

I don't smoke, I said.

He pointed back towards the alley behind the amusements. There's Dundrug's Casanova himself, hi. Constant woman supply. Kind of industrial strength, I offered.

It's cos he's blond, said Mustapha. Viking blood. Sailing the estuaries and setting the monasteries on fire. Chicks like that.

Chicks like guys what chop monks' heads off?

Chicks love power. You never watch films in yer life? Come here, how'd you think blond hair'd suit me?

I looked at Mustapha. His hair was blue black, his eyes dark so you couldn't even see the pupils and he smelled of a perfume appropriately entitled Axe.

He'd got the Mustapha handle cos his folks had the pallor of spuds sprouting in yer basement so either it was a recessive gene or else great dictator Saddam Hussein was his Da, though you wouldn't have said that to his face.

Aye, it'd suit you fine, I said.

Do you have a pound on you by the way?

For the hair consultancy, like?

Ah go on spot us an old government grant there. I seen you are after winning a twenty spot. Share the wealth, like.

I gave Mustapha a pound. If it meant I didn't end up with my mouth wrapped around one of his Doc Martens, fine.

He slipped off the car bonnet and headed for the cash desk inside the amusements. I saw him exchange the pound for a flowerpot of tuppence pieces, make for a slot machine, and, two minutes later, giving it a head butt.

I stood up and crossed the street.

But I heard McHugh calling me. By some strange circumambulation, he'd ended up outside of Top Sounds, was nubbing his phone off.

The crime? he said, pointing at my secret pocket.

24

Not tonight.

We headed back down past the tourist office, just as a guard car pulled up in front.

Teabags Malone was sitting on the ledge there talking to a German couple. Tall trim beings of a golden skin, golden hair and two bolts of unworldly blue eyes, they looked like they'd just got off their spaceship from the year 3058 when all facial aberrations will have been abolished, so they believed Teabags was Our Leader.

Bad fer the image of Dundrug, said Teabags, pointing scandalised at the American confederate flag whipping in the wind where the Union Jack used to be.

Alabama racists being more noble allies than the Brits, like!

The Germans tourists looked at the poster behind Teabags. And PJ Burren, who is he? the man asked.

Me cousin German, said Teabags.

Garda Mulligan walked up after appraising the substitution of the national flag. And what might you be doing here, Master Malone, he said.

Teabags looks at a point between his Doc Martens. Selling drugs, he said.

Oho, said the guard, and walked away.

Teabags pressed the right nostril on his big thick conk, and pushed a ball of snatter out of the left one. I reckoned that amongst our first ancestors on the African savannah there must have been cavemen with conks like that too. Maybe they even performed the same gestures.

The Germans went away and stopped in front of Dundrug's one pair of traffic lights which clicked amber all the time so they didn't know whether to stop or go.

Them Germans was on about the prehistoric cave paintings

near these parts, said Teabags. You ever heard of that?

Nyet, said McHugh.

Aye well, he showed me his map and says you go into them caves ye can see into the beginning of time, wee archers skittering down a wall after some buffalo like red fucking Indians. Thought of asking him for a spot of Red Leb but don't think he would've got the idea, just too healthy looking by far.

You PJ Burren's cousin? said McHugh.

Aye, gave him the idea for My Darling of Dundrug. The first line and all. Not seeing any royalties like. How are you, Hedgehog on Stilts?

Fine, I said.

Said Teabags, I'm a big fan of Germans personally though they are guilty of great crimes. Fr'instance ye can tell them stuff about spirits and goblins and fairy trees and they don't tell you to fuck off.

Myself and McHugh walked home and as he turned the key in the lock of his folks' house he put his hand into his pocket and handed me the Fractured Jehovah album that I was supposed to have swiped at Top Sounds.

Knew you'd chicken out, he said.

I pocketed the album. You going out late?

What's that to you?

Just asking.

Are the symptoms persisting?

What ones?

I'll tell her you said Hallo, if you want.

Aye, well, I reckon she plays in the Premier, if you know what I mean.

No I don't, but I reckon Little Lord Oyster's Dick doesn't get out at night cos Mammy says it's *wong*.

26

I reckon your whelk-covered stump is about to snap off the next time you molest it, I said, wiggling my wee finger.

Wanna bet on it?

Bet what?

Twenty pound I don't shag her this very night?

I could feel I was breaking into a sweat. I took the twenty I'd won from the poker, crumpled it up and kicked it into the street.

Twenty pounds say good luck there now, I said to him.

Which is when a car just sort of came flying up the road and drove over it.

McHugh joined his hands together and put them against his forehead like a Thai Buddhist and I was hoping he'd have an accident as he crept out his bedroom window that evening.

Not hair dye, not money, not charm, not brains, it was luck I needed.

I went off, headed into the middle of the street and picked the flattened twenty up.

Maybe I should have just bribed him to stay away from her, like.

I decided to avoid the new road whose neon lights had introduced a touch of suburbia to our lives but most importantly you could get your head kicked in more easily out there by the caravan sites. Instead, I went along the cliff walk. Through real country-style night I skulked past a rain shelter where there was a couple kissing beneath the legend Up the Provos scratched out in the pebbledash and I hoped it wasn't Her.

Then I cut on through Frankie Bullen's field where his Friesians grazed during the summer. As if they'd agreed on some robot signal, they all pulled themselves up by the forelegs, vast behinds rising in the field lit up by speckles of daisies, necks whirring left to greet my entrance into their lives while I headed for the cliff edge and sat down on an outcrop which gave onto giant black rectangular rocks below.

Cows were really freaky. You wondered how much of them was just programmed. But then I wondered how much of my own stuff was just programmed. Like about Her. Like why I was stirred up inside. By Her.

How much of yerself is all dog, I wondered, or cow or even sandpiper, scuttling back and forth whichever way the sea is going.

All the animal world just reacting to stuff, like when I was a kid I saw a poodle on the Tube in London barking at some flies, and my Da laughing at him, though sympathetically, cos maybe he understood the poodle.

I belly flopped onto the tufty grass on the cliff edge, and stared at this cluster of harebells just sprouted out of the side of the cliff, all asleep, and with my forefinger prodded at their silky wee heads a second. The wind was down, so it was all so quiet out there it was as though the stars millions of miles up even made a sound – like when you take a spoon to a wine glass and hit it a small tap. All the star stuff up there that we're supposed to be made out of, so we breathe like stars do.

So maybe the way stars produce light despite themselves, we're producing head thoughts, all a-flicker and forever changing shapes like flames. For instance, there's moments when I want to focus in on a differential calculus problem or something, but the figures get sucked into a wee mental mouse hole out of which, by way of compensation, them women from ABBA singing Dancing Queen, Dancing Queen slip out.

–Dancing Queen!

You're some mentaller, I said, and plucked a harebell and stuck it in my mouth. I zoomed in on the sea below, mellowed out, just slurping up along the giant blunt rocks and subsiding with a vast sigh and cider fizz.

The waves the waves, I muttered to myself, then I looked round, just to check if anyone were listening and taking notes on my pre-psychotic state.

Then I copped the rocks again, the way like Easter Island heads they were looking out to the horizon as though awaiting further instructions. Just like the gulls perched atop them.

I looked behind. I traced out Orion come up over Tievebawn mountain, the Dog Star pricking over the IRA summit. The Greeks! When they went into battle they gave long speeches, hacked their enemies' heads off and got a total rush out of it, the blood steaming off their limbs, their enemies crumpling to the ground like broken puppets. No problem for them.

As for me, I felt like the end of the line, cos I'd been in exactly one scrap in the last four years, and it was, to my eternal shame, against Squarehead O'Rourke, who introduced me to the taste of grass, which, as I lay face down on the football field, he invited me to eat. No problem for Squarehead either, but the speech he made about my impending doom due to grass suffocation wasn't in hexameters, understand.

Then there was one night after the disco when McHugh asked me if I was ready. Some lads had been troubling his woman, had knocked a pint over her skirt. So outside Fallon's chip shop he handed me a bed spring and said, You take out the fat one.

I am ready, I said.

I walked behind McHugh as he jumped a guy eating curried chips outside the amusement arcade. Then I noticed his fat friend was wearing spikes in his hair too. As McHugh and the other guy rolled about the footpath, the fat guy asked if I'd been listening to Fractured Jehovah's last album and we got talking.

Afterwards McHugh said to me, You goddamned chicken,

but I swear, even prior to fraternising with the enemy, like, the bed spring didn't stop trembling in my hands.

It had a life of its own.

I stood up, headed back for the cliff walk. That's when I felt my heart go on off in my chest cos like some animal I'd picked up that there was something alive out there amongst us without seeing it.

Looking southways I made out a figure in the distance, standing looking over the cliffs.

I started walking fast. There was like a drop-down list of potential assailants in my head. At the top was Mustapha Moran.

So out in that darkness I spontaneously started whistling My Darling of Dundrug, as if PJ Burren's romantic ooze could ward off evil spirits.

But the stranger started whistling the song too, and I started planning an exit, like throwing myself fast through the ditch in front of the holiday bungalows.

I was looking down on the ground as the stranger passed when I heard, Ah Jerome, it's yerself you frightened me there, and a hand reached out and touched me on the shoulder.

I turned and focused in on Ma McHugh.

She was wearing a long black coat and a black hat on her head, her blonde hair looking fresh washed the way it spilled down her shoulders sort of Victorian and abundant like.

I'm a bit of a cat, she said, I like to go out and prowl!

I'd never met her within a two-foot radius of The Chemist, so I was somewhat at a loss for words.

Won twenty pounds on the poker, I said, my voice coming out a couple of octaves higher than usual.

Were you lucky in other departments? she said, nodding towards the rain shelter.

I just came up to look at the sea.

I love them rocks below, you know the tall black ones.

Yes, I offered. They're sort of alive.

Yes alive.

The surface temperature of my cheeks must have been up to a hundred degrees Celsius. Then I blurted, It's like the ape sequence in 2001.

Come again?

The apes are starving, haven't a clue what to do and all. One morning Bingo, a black stone appears. And helps them evolve into men?

I don't know that film, she said.

So you understand that the stone's sent by a higher intelligence that's going to help them. Evolve into homo sapiens, like, evolve into us.

I put my hands in my pockets and looked off down the side of the hill at the squat off-white bungalows that were the acme of Dundrug civilisation.

What do you plan on studying when you leave town?

Don't know. Might do Philosophy.

Why that?

To expand my mind, I said, gulping.

She put her hand to my cheek and then she walked away.

Must look at those stones a bit more, get some ideas myself! she called.

With the trace of her fingers across my cheek I watched her leave and wondered if she'd been thinking of jumping or something, then I went to the edge of the cliff to cop the black monoliths below.

I stared at them a while like the monkey in 2001.

Then I knew what I had to do.

Cos it'd suddenly occurred to me that the principle underlying the universe was sex.

And I had to obey.

Part Two

1.

I awoke thinking about the time I was up in Saint Patrick's Purgatory at Lough Derg, walking barefoot about the gravel circles and trying not to stare too boggle-eyed at a coach-load of women from Lisnakool and environs who, like me, were up on this retreat ostensibly to get a couple of hundred years' indulgence so as to arrive in heaven quicker but actually just to check out the talent.

Following us about was this electric-guitar-playing priest just back from Africa after saving a tribe of pygmies in the Congo, telling us that hell wouldn't be that blast furnace of yore.

No stench, no cackling demons roasting ye over a spit lads, he said, but most likely just a kind of absence of God!

And McHugh, who was on the same trip, muttered that we must be living in hell already.

Until then I'd thought he was but some glamour-puss of a

skirt chaser deficient brain-cell-wise but it was from then on I started listening to him.

As we turned about the purgatorial circles he said it'd be more craic if the Greek gods in togas and braids were watching over us.

The Greek gods, he said, shagged like mad, drank like troopers, and they were really cool in them Italian films, hanging out in lofty marble rooms up on Mount Olympus.

Where he'd been with his old man.

It's like the world's one giant Risk board, he said. They push you here and there towards yer fate. They push some bucks towards a killing doom. And there's nothing much they can do about it.

They were certainly more laughs than our own God, who late twentieth century was sort of mellowed out and ready for a chat and gave you a hand with school exams and such.

He was like a cosmic PJ Burren gazing over all creation, saying, Now's the time for a nice cup of tea.

Whereas that weekend, it really felt like the wild beard Greek bucks were pushing Father Electric Guitar's button somewhere cos when the Lisnakool women slinked past him yelling Howya Father! his eyes went all starey and he took big great gulps of the ash-coloured Lough Derg air.

About a year later Mustapha Moran said he'd seen him in a pub in Blasnagall hanging out in denims and his hair in dreads with a six-foot-tall Congolese chick who spoke to him in some far out language with clicks and whirrs.

Over later games of Risk myself and McHugh gave Father Guitar's memory the thumbs up, but this morning as I opened my eyes and watched my wee sisters Emer and Maeve throw a pair of dolls out the bedroom window, I was wondering whether it was true, that riff we had about the priest.

Okay, I didn't believe in spirits or nothing, but it was like I'd been hit the night before.

Dundrug wasn't exactly Arcadia and yet it was like a couple of love arrows had struck me in the gut so I felt drunk, reluctant, and my heart was pounding, and even if I was going to make a total loser of myself, it didn't matter much.

It was like I was being pushed Siobhan-wards, whatever happened.

I got out of bed and threw on a bathrobe like Socrates prior to going to the agora. This being the twentieth century and July though, I was somewhere in Ireland in a bedroom on the ground floor I shared with two toddlers and one other sister Niamh, cos our chambers upstairs were given up to Northerners, Americanos and Germans and whoever was on for a spot of B and B.

No hope of enticing a night of love from some woman with such an arrangement, but never mind, I had other plans.

Out the window two of Frankie Bullen's Friesians were grazing on the flat electric green lawns of the new holiday bungalows, and another was slobbing a great big pie out onto the tarmac driveway. It hit the ground, and lay there all steaming and fresh.

Weird, but it was the second time this'd happened in the last month. About a week back, down at the posh new development by the dunes folk had woken up with half a dozen bullocks having a go at Petey O'Reilly's bread van. The local paper, the Dundrug Observer, was saying these cattle were being released by outside elements hell bent on sabotaging the town's reputation as Ireland's premium holiday resort.

As if!

I had nothing against progress, me, but still, I missed them fields that used to lie around us. Didn't mind the waft of cows either.

So I shrugged and pushed the bathroom door open and turned around Niamh who was bent over the sink.

Get out, she said.

Niamh had a twelve month lag on me, but she was a straight A student big into the local debating society, where she won prizes on the problem of masculinity and how Woman was better equipped to rule the world, theories that used to go down like a mug of cold sick in the old days, but were oh so cool now.

Still, I wondered whether her disparaging opinions were due to close contact with me!

All her friends were of the same sharpness, only they were posh dune residents, mouths full of braces and heads full of ponies.

Whenever I hung around, wanting to gawp at these self confident women destined for Harvard and jobs in the UN or something, they rolled their eyes and made me feel kind of autistic, underdeveloped, futile like some member of a race that had exhausted its genius.

Like men, I guess.

Why should I get out? I said.

Cos I'm bulimic and I'm secretly throwing up.

Hold on, I said, there's trickles of toothpaste going down the side of yer mouth.

And so?

Don't know. Makes you look like Dracula.

Out.

I want to ablute myself.

Ablute yerself upstairs I can smell you from here. How's the love life?

Exactly, I need yer advice.

You don't need advice, you need spray. Been slopping out in the byre recently?

Ach, you know yerself.

Ach sure I know, men in these parts couldn't wrestle a chicken if you paid them.

Feminist or not, she was still going out with Raymond Sweeney, the hotel owner's Gaelic playing son, who, with his huge fists and his hair which rose up from his forehead like porcupine quills, was only slightly less scary than Mustapha Moran.

I sprinkled water on my face, made a sign of the cross over her head, and swung towards the kitchen where a middle-aged man was cutting into a slice of black pudding, and a woman was standing over him with a pot of tea and they looked like some Dutch painting from the sixteenth century.

Anyone noticed the cows? I offered.

Neither heard me.

Da's knife scratched over the plate. Two slices of toast jerked up.

They didn't wake you, said Ma.

Atom bombs wouldn't wake that man up, said Da.

I leaned over and snatched the two squares of toast out and cos I was in this dreamy mood the slices looked weird, so I turned one round and round marvelling at its geometrical perfection.

Such were the discoveries I wanted to share with Her.

There was this noise at about half past two, said Ma, and wasn't it two pieces of Belfast skitter fighting and your father had to go up to them. And didn't one have his hands on the other's throat and was trying to squeeze the air out of him. What do you think of that?

What should I think? I sighed.

Well, it was just two cubs, said Da, peeping over the lip of his cup onto the surface of his tea.

But I knew something like that'd happen, said Ma.

Why that? I said.

The father has his head shaved. So did them skitters. And in terms of make up and bottles of peroxide the mother wasn't far behind in the social comment stakes.

Are ye criticising our brothers and sisters from the North?

Ah sure you know I wear the green like the next woman, but still.

And you took them in.

Need money to finance yer Bohemian lifestyle, don't we. Speaking of which, German man comes out onto the landing saying there were Inhabitual Noise just wearing a towel about his loins like Tarzan. Inhabitual, those were his words, do you mind. He looks at your father holding the Belfast skitters by the lugs and then goes back into the room. This morning his wife said she only heard the wind. What wind are you on about, I said, in my head but. She said it was beautiful. Why do Germans say such things? Is there no wind in Frankfurt?

Northerners still in bed? said Da.

May they sleep sound as babes, said Ma. Cos when they get up I have a wee bone to pick.

She laid down her dish cloth and picked up a pair of binoculars on top of the fridge, pointing them at the cliffs.

Has the invasion begun, said Da.

Can never be too sure this time of year, she said. Stabbings, fighting, young lads drowning in an ocean of Harp lager, it's like the Black Hole of Calcutta out there, times two. Oh look there's cows sabotaging at the holiday bungalows.

Ma put the binoculars down. Frankie Bullen's the latest victim, she said.

She giggled.

There was a moment of silence, so we homed in on the radio. There'd been an earthquake in Turkey, a train crash in India, some rioting in Belfast, Derry, the cities.

And just in, the newsreader intoned, the unstable blue giant star Sirius, commonly known as the Dog Star, has exploded.

The blast radius is thirty light years wide.

Earth is only ten light years away.

So we're doomed!

Okay, the last item's not true.

I looked at Da a second and it struck me that when he was born Adolf Hitler was still alive and I wondered whether that had impacted on his feelings, the way, like, we still breathe the same air Julius Caesar breathed. Or something.

What? he said.

Any chance of my getting out to the disco tonight? I said.

He looked into his teacup and gave it a whirl.

Nope, he said.

On what grounds? I said.

Ask your mother.

No on the same grounds as yer father, she said.

They snickered about their efficiency a second.

So be it, I sighed.

So be what?

Nothing, I said.

But now that permission was not forthcoming, Plan B was forming in my mind, which is to say, doing a McHugh out the window. With Da's ladder.

Niamh pushed open the door and sat down opposite me as the Angelus bell began donging on the radio.

Hail feck full of feck the Lord is with feck, she chanted.

Da said, What's the matter, sweetheart. Got something

39

against the Virgin Mary?

Niamh put her head in her hands and said, Ah Daddy you're ancient and venerable enough to know it's all a great lie.

You split up with Raymond Sweeney again?

Don't think that's the appropriate question. What's Granny doing out in our field by the way?

Wants to look at the mountain.

Bit far from London the mountain, in't it?

She came back.

Wish I was in London.

What did you say, sweetheart?

Nothing, though I just sometimes identify with transsexuals. Why's that?

Cos transsexuals feel like women born in men's bodies. And I feel like I'm from London, except I'm here.

Then just like Adolf Hitler she pointed her finger at the ground in this nervy, kind of spastic way.

Here! she said.

It must have been the debating society.

Then she turned on me. What's the matter with you? she said. Unless it's some gloopy poem you want me to read again about yer imaginary girlfriends.

I would usually have taken up on such provocations, but I just smiled at her with my mouth full of toast.

And then I did my Ray Sweeney impersonation.

I collapsed on the floor, dragging my knuckles along the linoleum and grunting.

Niamh I fucking love you, I sobbed.

Da stood up. Well, someone's got to toil.

He picked his master keys out of the drawer and said, Say hallo to yer grandmother by the way.

Niamh put her head in her hands and said, What would you do if I said I was a transsexual called Rupert by the way?

Da clipped his keys onto his belt buckle.

I guess I'd say Okay... Rupert.

After I'd eaten I dootered out in my Socrates gown to the garden, unwrapping the Fractured Jehovah *Crolly Doll Massacres* CD. I planned to pore long and lovingly over Jugger Zoltan and the boys' incoherent album notes (all praise to interstellar vibes etc...) prior to ratcheting up the bedroom hi-fi to full bass busting thunder for half an hour as one way of blanking out thoughts of love.

Thoughts of Her.

But first Granny, who'd be glad for the Padre Pio snap which I'd taken also.

Like she'd been lowered down from out of the sky by a team of sprites, she was in the field sitting in an antique armchair Da had upholstered with pink velvet and white tassels. We used to call it the Marie Antoinette chair until Granny had taken a shine to it. The grass was all waist high and swaying in the breeze about her cos Da liked to let it grow. Come autumn he would scythe, bale and sell it to Frankie Bullen, the current victim of anti Dundrug saboteurs.

But I reckon it was also cos Da was a bogman from Dunfagart and he liked the weirdness of real grass, the stalks with furry black tops or crumbly white flowers that looked like oats, cos all around grew the industrial variant which was sort of billiard table green and samey.

Hiya Granny, I said.

Granny came from this other time when women used to have tons of nippers and men sat in front of the turf fire silent and philosophical. One day we'd driven *en famille* up the back roads behind Dunfagart and Da pulled up in front of this three room cottage standing on a slope which was covered in rocks and pebbles all the way up to the black summit. It was so quiet you could hear your ears buzz, and the sheep like a mystery tribe all amber-eyed and carpety heads closed in as if they wished to articulate the woes of sheepness to us.

Da said, This is where I grew up, and the wee ones Emer and Maeve burst into tears. I climbed over the half door and checked out the room where Granny had given birth to a dozen kids, and in this kind of shattering silence of rock and inarticulate sheep I tried to work out where I came from – from him, from Ma, and from this ancient red head woman.

Who was sitting right now commanding a view of the field, the Ballytubber road, the purple bogland beyond.

But she was looking at Tievebawn the way she usually did, quietly, fixedly, like she could catch it erode.

And Tievebawn was looking back at her, cos mountains catch human erosion faster.

There was a filterless cigarette smouldering between her lips. There were only a few shops now that sold her Players Navy Cut, which gave off these creamy dense fumes that smelled of the room back in Dunfagart.

I stood there a second watching her as the coal turned orange and then smoke issued from her nostrils as though she were breathing along with the mountain.

Before the coal flared up again, I bent over, kissed her forehead, sat down in the grass, and said, So you're here.

Ah Michael you're late.

It's Jerome.

Are you Jerome?

Yes.

She squinted her eyes up as if she didn't quite believe me.

I left yer Aunt Kathleen's place, she said. There was her childer flying around, so I required more peace. What happened with yer hair it's standing in a funny shape.

I just woke up, I said.

I saw one of them rock and roll men on the TV that wears lipstick and his hair like yours, a pineapple, and he said he weren't, you know... queer?

I showed her the front cover of the Fractured Jehovah album. Jugger Zoltan! I said.

You wouldn't flatten it with a bit of Brylcreem, would you.

I'd rather saw off my leg.

Don't say that, it could happen.

I pulled the Padre Pio hologram from my bathrobe. Can I interest you in a saint? I said.

You need it more than I do, she said. You could pray that you'll find a nice lassie. You're a terrible one for the dancing and the fights.

No I'm not. That was Michael.

Though I do not know if Padre Pio is one for the lovers, for some say his ones don't work with carnal things. I tried, and there's no power to them.

I tilted the hologram a bit to get the close up on old Daddy Pio's scabs, and I felt a chill go up my back, a chill that said that unless the nutter had been gouging out bits of his own hands for that full-on Christ experience, all knowledge of science weren't going to help explain the big scabby nuggets... on his hands!

I saw Father McNulty walking his dog Jack, she said. And sure he has no power left either.

How that?

Cos there was Northern ones from the caravan site shouting

43

You child molester at him I swear and if you cursed a priest in my day you'd drop dead that evening. In great agony too.

We watched as a blackbird hopped along the front wall with a worm in its beak.

Maybe they're dead right now? I said.

She blessed herself. Don't say that it might happen, and that blackbird is bad news as far I am concerned.

Aye, Granny were about as Christian as a druid poring over chicken guts, Salisbury Plain, circa 1000 BC. She read tea leaves, saw signs in clouds, and thought birds whacking into a window were evil portents, particularly for the Maguires. Her head must have been one vast Louvre, I thought, aglow with lost atmospheres that books don't catch.

Only I often had trouble understanding her. But I could always try, so, very sensitively, I said, Did you see anyone get killed in the war of Independence?

Why do you ask?

Just historical-minded me. Did the Black and Tans burn down yer house?

They didn't. A priest had blessed it. So they were standing behind my father's gate when I was twelve and they didn't go any further, but they were fine looking Englishmen with green eyes I had never seen the like of. A blond one with buck teeth gave me thruppence and the next day The Boys shot them both.

She touched her temple. In the back of the head, and there was crimson stains at the front of the barracks that you couldn't wash out, she said. But my Daddy said it was best they were dead them being foreign invaders and Ireland unfree and so I buried the thruppence after that and forgave them.

Who, the Boys?

No, them English bastards.

She covered her face in her hands and said, You look like my brother Michael, dead these thirty years.

I got the chills, stood up, waved at her, and went back to the bedroom to listen to Jugger Zoltan and the boys. Out the window Ma was in the back yard shaking a stick at Frankie Bullen's cattle who were making a bid to break across the wall and eat the abandoned dolls.

No chance of music though, cause Niamh, standing between me and my breeches, was teaching the wee ones new crimes to inflict on their Lego Men.

This is what you get for yer radical subversion, she said, in an accent which was supposed to come across as Latin American but which to my ear sounded Pakistani.

I looked up as she lofted the helicopter and out fell a Lego left wing activist pushed by a Lego policeman.

The girls squealed and said, Kill him again!

I grunted at Niamh and pointed at my jeans, which she pulled from the chair and tossed across the room so in one heart stopping moment I saw my twenty pound note, house key, poem notebook and the single rubber arc across the room and hit Emer on the head.

I dived for the rubber before Emer could pick it up and, who knows, swallow it.

Niamh said, What's that you've dropped.

Nothing, I answered, what's wrong with you.

I picked up the rubber and shoved it into my jeans, tried to insert my right foot into right leg of said article but instead just seemed to collide with the door put there deliberately to impede my progress. I said Ha, ha, as though that had been part of my plan then headed for the door, the jeans stuck around my ankle, and with a sudden slump sensation in the gut I wondered, Did

Stud McHugh have need to use his rubber last night?

Give us a look, said Niamh.

A look at what, I said.

I know what you're after picking up. And I really have to laugh. You only got one?

I picked up my money. You're hallucinating; this is really mad, Niamh.

The light streaming through the window caught a gloop of snot on Maeve's arm. Emer cradled a decapitated Barbie and said, Do you have some sweets?

Then she looked into the Barbie's neck cos, believe me, there's something like a strain of dementia in small children.

Those aren't sweets big brother's got, said Niamh, drawing Emer close to her. Oh no!

What are they then?

Ask him.

Emer put her arms around my leg and said, What do you have in your pocket?

I took out a fifty pence piece and stuck it into her doll's neck. Get big sister Niamh some skag with that, I said.

It was opportune to get the hell away.

Jerome? said the sister.

I turned. Aye?

Who's the lucky squirrel?

She came out with a piratical laugh. The psycho wee ones joined her.

I didn't bother answer that, for I could no longer be worried for such trivial things.

I had to plot my tasks ahead.

My mind on love.

My mind on war.

2.

Now picture that the sun, lobbed way up in the sky earlier, had spun in a downward curve towards the mid Atlantic. The light was getting a tad bit fizzy. Evening meals had been consumed, shopping expeditions performed, the empty beach was settling into being itself, just waves slopping up, waves sliding back. Brown and black cattle lowed in the fields waiting for broad backed farmers (with tits) to milk them and McHugh was poring over the Risk board like a Greek God on the skids.

Some time after eight o'clock.

He gave the table a kick, clenched his fists vowing exactions, but nothing except a last minute thunderbolt headed my way was going to save his Irish Empire sandwiched in the plains of Arkansas, nor were there any divine powers ready to bail out the last dribbles of the green generations scuttling down to the darkest Congo or holding out in the Isles of Japan.

Say your prayers, I said, cos when the Soviet Union rolls into town, Religion's officially abolished, like! Though I was only in half-gloat mode right then because so far he'd been reluctant to fill me in on the previous night's doings. So when I taunted him there was something of a muffled interrogative sob in my voice, and my leg was going jig jig under the table.

I rolled the dice, double sixes and a five.

McHugh cursed, threw, then scooped up another half dozen dead regiments.

No justice left in this world, he muttered. No sir.

I picked up the dice to start a clean up job in the Congo.

She believes you're interesting, he said.

I flung the dice across the board but somehow they fell off the table.

47

What's that supposed to mean.

I didn't ask. I was sitting on the beach with her. Waves were lapping in great lascivious tongues upon the strand while this groovy minstrel wearing shades, though it's dark, Brian Sweeney, like, was playing his twelve string guitar and humming Hotel California and she declared – JEROME. INTERESTING.

I gave the table a kick and tendered him the dice. Sorry, I said, but would you care to throw these or are you totally awash in yer self love?

McHugh picked up the dice and blew on them. Now as for me, I'm not interesting at all, he said.

Well thank God somebody's noticed. Throw?

Shaking the dice slowly in his hands he said, I'm obscure, apparently.

You obscure.

Aye, a Rebel, a Vagabond... a Gypsy. Like a Russian.

He threw the dice across the board. His three fives ate into my Congo pincer movement, and there was something like a sense of doom in the pit of my guts.

Like a Russian?

Aye, like some bloke Alosha or Alexei who stabs his Da, marries a prostitute and slams a door on his hand to prove his love.

She said that about Finbar McHugh from Dundrug?

Must have been well after two in the morning. Must have been stoned. I resign, by the way.

What do you mean resign.

Exactly what the word means, he said. Resign. I withdraw. The game's kaput.

McHugh must have had his Way with her, I was thinking, as I looked at the great swathe of communist subversion that

Interesting Jerome Maguire had sown across the globe, and it hit me that maybe all those sleepless crazies, like Stalin or Mussolini fr'instance, those who ground up generations of human bone and meal in the cogs of history, might have had disappointing adolescences like me.

I've never resigned, I said.

Well that's your prerogative.

I got up out of the chair and went over to the window, my eyes riveted to the ground, anywhere but in McHugh's direction. I drew the window up, stuck my head out, and it was all the same whether it didn't fall back down and lop my head off, a rain of carotid blood spattering the car bonnets below, the masses cheering.

Cos I'd have exchanged my head to have been in McHugh's place. Aristo-murdering Robespierre, as the guillotine blade sliced through his neck, must have had a similar reflection. He'd only been a bastard cos the women found him Interesting.

Right, we're going out then? said McHugh.

I pulled my coat on. Go out where?

Timbuktu. I don't know. What are the options.

He opened the door and said, I'll be back in a minute.

I shuffled across the empty room and pored over the Risk board and shovelled the Red army into the Congo. Meanwhile, old David Bowie was on the turntable warbling another dirge about his bendy depraved existence in Berlin and instead of thinking He Is So Cool, he was actually starting to depress me totally.

There was a knock on the door.

It weren't David Bowie about to take issue with my sentiments, but surprise, Ma McHugh.

Though she was looking utter class in a black catsuit with white pearls clicking around her neck, she'd only have had to put on a mask and she'd have been a member of some highly paid assassination squad that killed foreign diplomats with Kung Fu kicks leaving no bruises.

Love is in the air yippee yi yay, in't it? she said.

What?

You know the song. Love Is in the Air?

I have absolutely no idea, I said.

Ye boys on the tear tonight?

Not sure.

Here's a gloomy man. Didn't them rocks have all the answers? she said.

I looked up at her, just as she winked at me.

Mrs McHugh you are very elegant, I said.

I look what?

I said Elegant.

Thanks.

I was only just saying it, like.

Did you never learn not to retract compliments?

She walked over to the table and put her hand on my shoulder.

Going to the Mass in Main Street again?

I looked up at this sexually mature forty-year-old woman who was winding me up and all I could say was, Mrs McHugh I do not believe in God.

You're some obscure one, she said, giving my head a rub, thus ruining my spikes. And Finbar always said you were religious. Didn't you write some story about Jesus once?

Aye, when he goes to Mars and converts a tribe of six foot cockroaches. I was eight.

There you go, you still have the faith, she said, flicking her lighter on, applying it to the tip of her Rothmans Extra, from which a wee lump of a flame came out.

Anyway, she said, we're off to another sort of Mass. PJ Burren's homecoming concert! At the Star of the Sea. Is that your money?

I looked on the table where she pointed and there was a crumpled up twenty pound note there.

Finbar's Da likes him, she said. Soothes his nerves, so he says. More like he's soothing PJ's wallet but. Where's Finbar gone?

Bedroom, I said, unfolding the note and I'd never thought I'd be so happy to be gazing on the monocled WB Yeats.

Look after him, will you?

Look after Finbar?

He's in trouble, Jerome, she said.

He's what?

And we all know you're a bit wild sometimes. Like all free thinkers.

I weren't really listening to her, so rapt was I by the sight of the twenty pound note. So when I looked up to make sure I'd heard right the free thinker comment there was only a puff of smoke left cos she'd already gone.

My heart was pounding and my head spun as I headed out to the stairs.

McHugh was standing on the landing checking himself out in the mirror. You chatting my Ma up?

What sort of shite do you fill her with? I said.

No idea what you're on about. Did ye find yer money?

I didn't make no bet with you either.

Yes you did though the Greek gods tell us it is bad to bet on women.

Oh aye, so what happened?

Don't remember much. I had a toke on a joint and suddenly everything goes recto verso and next thing I'm crawling along the sand. Take these, by the way.

He handed me a pair of wire cutters.

We planning to escape from Dundrug tonight? I said, slipping them into my secret pocket.

Security purposes.

We slid down the banisters for the street door and did a ninety degree veer Timbuktu-wards.

Green, violet and orange streaks streamed out in that upended bowl of blue which was our portion of Irish sky with swallows swarming all black against the light. Everything looked so still, but I wondered whether, just by concentrating hard enough, I could feel the hurtling of the world, the Japanese bullet train speed of us through Space.

And beneath the swallow swarm negotiating the world's crust atop six inch platforms, two caravan site girls slugged on a cider bottle and sang My Darling of Dundrug.

All cos fever was coming on again.

But this night fever was mine!

And it's funny, said McHugh, cos it was coming out of my nose and the sand was sparkling beneath me, and I felt like an animal. A lizard, that must be my totem, like.

I was trying not to sound too happy, but I still said, More like a crocodile, you sot.

So I must have crawled a hundred yards cos I woke up in a golf bunker, and there was a car in it.

In yer dreams, I said.

No fucking joke. It was Crazy Nolan, the retired guard. Said he got lost on the way home from the club.

We were coming up to Main Street. You talk a lot of shite, McHugh, I said.

What sayest?

Shite.

McHugh pointed up the street. Would you ever check this out, he said.

I thought he was talking about Main Street, for it was packed, as if the entire North had come to town. But in fact he was pointing at a figure standing still in the middle of it all like some desert prophet – yer man who'd been kneeling before the BBQ café the night before.

His hands joined together, his Brazil shirt covered in stains, he was in fervent prayer while the crowd sought solutions as to how to get round him.

McHugh shook his head and said, Gregory, she ain't worth it!

The man called Gregory looked at him, shook his head, and then ran across the road yelling Leslie Leslie. He held his hand out at the trapped cars honking on Main Street.

Man drunk and dying of a broken heart due to some waitress, said McHugh shaking his head again, as we took our places up on a car bonnet to see what else Main Street would throw up.

Which was when a kid about four foot nought homed in on us with a Kiss Me Quick hat on his head, a cloud of freckles buzzing about on his nose but his eyes like two broken bits of blue glass really looking ancient already. Hey Mister, he said. Would you be wanting any plastic bullets. Sure go on they're only two pound.

McHugh pushed him aside so he could keep an eye on Gregory, who was now kneeling on the other side of the street. We've bullets enough, he said, staring straight ahead. Man was selling the same ones for twenty p last year.

That's inflation due to the attack of George Soros on the pound, lads, said the kid, but them were rubber ones, d'you see. But the plastic ones are yer real collector's items. This one hit a man fr'instance.

Just then Gregory dashed past us in a blur with his head down yelling Leslie Leslie.

Ah for Christ's sake, said the kid. It's only two pound.

It was looking as if Gregory was trying to bust open the BBQ front window, but just before his crown made contact with the glass he crumpled to the ground like an Italian in the penalty area.

McHugh said, If you stuck that bullet up your arse right now I'd give you ten.

The kid tapped his temple. You are a very sick man, he said. And then he walked off.

Why doesn't she want me any more? screamed Gregory, pulling at his teeshirt, as though it were smothering all the love parts of him, as though he were trying to get out of the body of himself, and all we could do was shrug.

Look out for yer jugular on the glass there Gregory, said McHugh.

Boss Cullen stepped out of the café and pulled Gregory up to his feet.

You're frightening my customers, he said.

She broke me heart, said Gregory and the tears were streaming out of his eyes.

Boss Cullen said, Gregory, would you ever act like a man.

Leslie, I'm a man! said Gregory. Then he ran back across the road.

Gregory was no oil painting. In fact he had this squashed up face and a mass of hair pouring out of his head like all the booze he was on nourished his follicles directly.

But still, I was sorry for him.

I scanned the street to see where Siobhan might be when I spotted this man skirting round Gregory and I said Polio, or MS? He was walking with his knees turned in, his canes going up and down like feelers, his eyes rolling.

You think that's a disease? said McHugh. That's The Boys.

How's that?

Yer man there won't be doing what he did again so quickly.

Is that a baseball bat job or do they still rely on the old breeze-blocks?

Those would be a picnic compared to how he's walking. Must have been peddling big drugs or something. Anti-social element, like.

The man crossed the street and walked by us half of his face carved flat at the cheekbone and we didn't say a word. He was staring at this invisible point he was trying to attain with legs and canes like on a medieval pageant.

Then he suddenly pulled up and turned right round.

What in fuck were you looking at? he said, his eyes going McHugh's way.

I didn't know what McHugh was feeling right then, but all the blood had left my head.

Nothing, said McHugh, his face flushed and with a weird smile. We were just chatting, like.

The man held his stick over McHugh's head. Like to see this sticking out of your eye socket for ye sins?

No, I wouldn't.

No sir, you wouldn't and why wouldn't you?

Cos it would hurt?

No it wouldn't hurt but you wouldn't look half so smart then, you laughing cunt.

Sorry.

Why are you sorry?

For looking at you, McHugh said, looking at the footpath.

You're going to be, said the man. And then with his evil

portents he set off again, a gangling set of black sticks and legs cutting an empty space for himself through the crowd.

Drug dealer, whispered McHugh.

Psycho, I said.

We were quiet a second in the midst of a thousand footfalls.

So do you know who The Boys are?

Take it easy, said McHugh, looking down the street.

Then he lit up a cigarette and blew out a big cone of blue smoke.

Aye, right, let me just give you their names and address first, he said. Which springtime gave birth to you, lad?

Just tell us about them, I said.

McHugh looked from left to right and then said he was in the North once for an internment commemoration rally and got talking to this man in a snazzy linen suit with black designer brogues that shone like LPs.

Those were real Eye-talian shoes, I swear, he said, and him buying rounds in the pub like there's no tomorrow and talking about his philosophy of life.

So he was one of The Boys, I said.

It got to about three in the morning, yer man in the suit sniffs a bottle of poppers and he just lies down in the middle of the road and he's not for getting up. Go way to fuck, he says. Picture a white linen suit and shiny shoes by the walls of Derry. When I pull him up off the ground all of a sudden he has his hands about my throat saying, Shut the fuck up okay.

McHugh's phone bleeped and he started texting someone.

That's what The Boys are sometimes like, he said.

Psycho as yer man with his sticks?

Maybe he's one of The Boys and he was blown up by his own bomb.

I let out a sigh, cos I'd had enough of McHugh and his

56

stories which turned in upon themselves endlessly.

So where's Siobhan? I said.

Who cares?

I'm interested.

She could be in darkest Africa with the wild beasts of the jungle for all I know. I said she was complicated.

I have a poem for her.

If there's one thing that's certain, said McHugh, it's that there's no sponds—

Aye right, I interrupted, and there was Gregory sitting on the footpath opposite, cross-legged and talking to the man with the sticks.

What's it about? he said, still texting all the time.

Stuff.

He looked at me. Stuff, he said, as though he knew exactly what stuff signified.

Tell me more about The Boys, I said.

McHugh looked at the two figures across the street. Later, he said, let's head.

We turned rapidly off towards the beach road and then there was this surge of sweet dread in my belly cos I spotted Siobhan on a car bonnet in front of the Stella Maris, and like on a tiny boat that's hit a ten footer, sea and sky just upended for a second.

Then I just cruised her way and McHugh, to piss me off, stuck his hands out and staggered like a zombie coming out of a tomb.

Uuuurgh, he said.

Shut up.

She was wearing a tight denim jacket and a Palestinian scarf about her head, smoking an Embassy Regal, a sandal dangling off her big toe. A girl who resembled her uncannily sat across from her on a window ledge wearing a tee-shirt which said

Hallo Cutey, a smiling pink cat emblazoned on it.

But as I was wearing a teeshirt which said Fashion is Death I had the last word.

Which was good, because I was feeling sort of speechless.

I stepped off the kerb to avoid a surge of farmers, nuns, the blind, the maimed, the faithful heading into the hotel for PJ Burren's Welcome Home concert, and like an unwelcome guest PJ's song had taken up residence in my head, except the lines had changed:

> *We'll get married on the strand*
> *And you will hold my gland*

...and I was afraid I just might blurt it out.

Meet my sister, Eileen.

Eileen pointed and said, You write poetry.

Who are your sources?

She swung her legs from the window ledge and said, Wee birds.

Siobhan pulled on her cigarette and with hooded Palestinian sort of eyes she looked at McHugh, who was hovering somewhere behind me.

Oh there's Lazarus risen from the dead, she said.

The sister swung her legs and said, He were scuttered bad last night!

Anyway, said Siobhan, youse are all acquainted now. See ye at Planet 2001 for the Skanky Malachy gig?

The sister swung her legs and said, Go on, it should be a great dance. Before the band comes on there's a DJ spinning eighties stuff and I was just a baby then!

She looked like someone'd just given her a big cheque for her confirmation.

I noticed the Tara ring on Siobhan's finger had the heart bit turning upwards which, in these parts, meant she was available!

Either that or PJ Burren, she said and winked.

I'll be there, I said, giving her my best Errol Flynn – all eyes a-twinkle and toothy guffaw after dispatching a load of pirates or something.

But the way I was feeling all dread and longing it was probably more Errol Flynn as child killer.

I waved and started walking home, McHugh swinging in beside me.

I said, I've got a devilish plan involving a ladder. What about you?

McHugh pulled a miniature whiskey bottle out of his pocket and he took a swig of it.

This might kill you, he said. Please try.

I took a swig out of the bottle. I buckled up and half of it came out of my nose.

What was that?

You know moonshine?

Aye?

That's black hole, man. Black hole.

I got home, catching a glimpse of the clan minus me zonked out in front of the telly in the living room. Like a shadow I clung to the back walls till I got to the kitchen window, where the ladder was, then ducked.

I raised my head straight up like a periscope and came face to face with Ma in the kitchen, her hands in a basin of fresh washed clothes. I was about to shift into Plan Z, and say Wahoh, surprise, at her, when I realised that she hadn't even seen me, was tuned into some private wavelength of her own. I ducked down again as she turned and headed out of the kitchen to the back door.

I scuttled for cover around by my bedroom wall, and crouched down. She was hanging wet white sheets up on the empty washing lines, and singing a song –

> *When we were savage, fierce and wild*
> *Whack for the diddle of the die do day*
> *She came like a mother to her child*
> *Whack for the diddle of the die do day*

I waited there a while listening to her sing. Okay, there was a clothes peg between her teeth, but put it like this, if Ma'd had to sing half decently to save the planet, you'd have to start building your escape rocket now. The white sheets slapped in the wind, and she was kinking her hips from side to side randily and I was sort of filled with a sense of biblical shame to witness her privacy so on my hunkers I crab-walked further into the shadows.

Which was when a tiny voice rang out in the night.

Mama!

I looked down and saw I'd stepped on Emer's doll, which was staring up at me with fluorescent blue eyes.

At the washing line, Ma stiffened, turned around and listened in.

But she only got Dundrug wind, though the way my heart was thumping in my chest, I was wondering if she could hear it. She went back inside. I headed back kitchen ways and hauled the ladder over so it rested beneath the bathroom window first floor. It was standing right by the folks' bedroom, but since the curtains were drawn and no one in Ireland particularly likes fresh air, the odds on those curtains coming back and my escape being discovered were sort of lengthy.

Then I was back in the living room.

Ma and Niamh were looking me up and down as though they'd rehearsed it, but Ma was trying to look serious. What's in your pockets? she said.

Nothing, are you going to search me or something?

I just might do that, she said, if I feel like it.

Niamh was smirking and I realised I'd have to review the occasional alliances I made with her against the folks and I drew my finger across my neck to indicate what evil fate awaited her.

Aye in yer dreams big boy, she said.

Ma tittered and twirled a glass of sherry in her hand, leaning forward a picture of alertness in her seat as she always did when she was happy.

Were you lucky, said Da.

They all started laughing.

Nope.

Come here till I see your lovebites.

No lovebites, I said.

No lovebites! Where's the lipstick on your collar then?

There's no lipstick.

And the money I gave you, where is it?

Inflation, I guess, I said, and then, just to be sure, I went – I suppose I'm not on dance permission yet?

Nope, said Da. How's town centre?

Oooh just the usual Henley regatta vibe.

I was edging towards the door. Well, I said, rubbing my hands, I think I shall retire from this scene of familial Irish bliss. Unless ye all want to listen to *Crolly Doll Massacres* sans earphones?

ALL: God bless us and save us.

On the way out I waved and said, I bid you g'night Granny.

By the door, she sat in the Marie Antoinette armchair, peering at world famous feminist Andrea Dworkin in blue dungarees and frizzy hair on the *Late Late Show* arguing like Niamh that women should rule the world, while Gay Byrne, the bollocks, was looking like she'd asked if anybody minds she farted.

Not that I thought that women wouldn't be just as crap as men ruling the world, mind.

But it was just that when anyone got an idea on the *Late Late Show*, Gay Byrne would always be winking like a goblin and inviting the Plain Folk in the audience to have a snicker at what thinkers thunk.

Oh hallo Michael, said Granny, you're back early for a change.

No one in the room corrected her.

You should do something with the hair Michael, she said, but sure you've always been the wild one.

Everyone in the room started concentrating on the *Late Late Show*, cos Granny had a habit of coming out with things lately and we all hoped it would pass.

She said, And you always said you'd drink a million pubs dry.

Then she snickered.

It's not Michael, said Da. It's Jerome.

Granny looked at me and squinted up her eyes, all suspicious again. Is that Jerome now?

It's Jerome Maguire, Granny.

Our son, said Ma.

I pulled out of the room again bidding all good night, headed down to the bedroom where the girls were fast asleep, their eyes scrunched tight and mouths wide open like scaldy birds, and giving off that smell which wasn't fags, booze, sweat, but came from the weird world of half-dreams and accumulated

62

knocks they lived in. I climbed onto the top bunk, and pushed pillows under the quilt and put a football in a pillow slip by way of representing my head, but as this semblance of a sleeping figure hadn't even worked for Clint Eastwood in *Escape from Alcatraz* I also had to ensure that the sister didn't squeal on me. I pulled out my poem notebook and started writing.

Dear Niamh, should you betray me this evening a great disaster will befall you such as Dundrug has never seen. Love, Jerome. PS Please accept a five pound bribe.

I left the note on her pillow and slipped out of the room. It was a cinch getting up the stairs, only fate had planted a German woman sitting on the landing to spoil my plans.

Do you hear the wind? she said.

I didn't even want to think of the reprisals should the folks discover my first ever escape job. Yeah, I whispered. Beautiful, i'nt it.

Why do you whisper? she said. Are you Irish?

Sort of.

Irish young people do not like the wind, usually. They do not like the mountains, which they find boring.

I thought about this a second, and I was feeling panicky, like my judgement and brain weren't co-ordinated.

Well, I'm sort of English too. In a way.

So why do you say me you are Irish?

Yes, I answered, waving at her, and walking into one of the guest rooms that had a key hanging out of the lock.

I thought of turning on the light a second but instead closed the door behind me and hoped the ethereal German would go floating back into poetic room 3 to admire the gooey pictures of tearful clowns and puppy dogs hanging from the walls.

I stood listening to the wind whispering off the windows a

bit, and right then the bedside lamp kicked on and it was the two kids who'd been scrapping the night before sitting up in a double bed and looking at me.

They both had on Celtic shirts out of which poked shaved round heads, their lugs sticking out of the sides like white flowers.

Mister we were only talking, said the eldest, who was about ten with scabs on his elbows.

What? I said.

We weren't fighting or nothing, I swear.

It took me a second for this to sink in. Then I said, Aye well I was just making sure cos if there's trouble I'll be back.

I promise we'll go to sleep.

The little one said, Hey Mister are you a pervert?

That's exactly it, I said, and went out the door, just as I heard the bathroom latch coming off.

I nipped across the corridor, and went into the airing cupboard while the Ma of the kids went back into the bedroom. The German had disappeared, so I slid into the bathroom, and my hands trembled as I tweaked a knob of gel into my spikes.

Then I was out the window and down the ladder, the ladder juddering, and for a second it felt as if I were descending into the bowels of hell and perdition cos in truth I'd just cut something with the family universe bound up within those four walls.

But I shook that sensation off, cos freedom had a good taste too, like the sip of an adult drink, and like my uncle Michael who I'd never met, I could drink a million pubs dry.

I headed for the cliffs, but then I stopped, looking back on to the new road, with its strip lights marking the smooth tarmac way into Dundrug. Across the lane, in the council estate, the night wind blowing in from the Atlantic drove a wheelie bin parked out for the evening along the footpath and it clunked into a council palm tree.

The wind blowing against the stars up on the cliff walk would have been something, but I had no time to lose. Nor did I care much if I ran into someone who would kick my brain out through my nose.

The road was smooth and black and led to love.

And this was my night of love after all.

I did a Kung Fu punch and set off.

3.

DJ Tingle of Planet 2001 was notorious in my family due to an incident involving my cousin Geraldine and a beach party up in Ballybobeg the summer before. All other details were *verboten*, but Ma considered Tingle the personification of Evil. As for me, I could not disagree with her on this point. With his hair tied up in a pony tail, his red spectacles, his fluorescent blue shirt, he looked like some nightmare of the future.

As I walked in, he turned down the sound on the eighties hit he was playing and everyone on the dance floor sang *Agadoo, doo, doo, push pineapple, shake a tree*, after which he groaned, Blast from the Past! into his microphone.

No one seemed bothered at all. Rather, songs like Agadoo by Black Lace made people happy.

With this gulag music in my ears I walked past the stage where roadies were stacking Skanky Malachy's amps and doling out lengths of cable and I weaved towards the bar for a drink. Bouncers were standing all over the place, huge men from off the mountains whose hump backs and glazed eyes promised a few minutes of mirthless brutality around the back should you so much as breathe near them. I got my elbows onto the bar, where Stephen Pugh, the thirteen-year-old barman wearing a dickie bow and white shirt, pulled me a pint of watery beer into a plastic container.

Good man, Jerome, it might never happen! he said.

I stood against a wall covered in glittery scales, nodding at Teabags and Punch Gilbride who were staring at a pair of peroxide women dancing about on huge platform heels. To the left, to the right, the women yelled, but Teabags and Punch only hovered tensed up against the wall, their eyes wide, mouths open, as if they'd just been born adult-sized and these were the first women they'd ever seen.

Siobhan's sister appeared, and she stood on her tip toes about an inch away, blinking her eyes real fast, her breath smelling of Kisscool chewing gum.

Where's Siobhan? I said.

She pointed back behind the DJ box and I sort of walked away without saying anything to her.

When I got to Siobhan the Intifada wear had given way to a black shiny number, and her hair was piled up with curls all spiralling down the nape of her neck. She looked so delicious that some weird instinct kicked in and I wanted to take a chunk out of her neck with my teeth.

It was as though there were this wild abundance inside, so I wondered whether I'd be able to hold onto myself for the next couple of hours as I loomed over her table holding my pint.

She patted a place beside her.

Where's McHugh? I said, into her ear as Eileen reappeared, sliding into a seat and bouncing along it until she was direct across, leaning over to be part of the conversation.

How am I supposed to know, I'm not telepathic.

Her lips brushed against my ear and every single hair on my neck could have been counted right at this moment. She offered a cigarette.

No thanks.

Oh it's a killer alright, she said, lighting up.

Will you dance?

Oh God, she said.

I take that as a no.

It's actually a yes, sort of.

Eileen leaned over and said, Do you know this song?

I said, Yes, and then, confused, took Siobhan's Pernod for my pint and drank it.

But there's a problem, said Siobhan. Kind of a music one.

I completely understand, I replied, re-appropriating my pint.

I'm beginning to think that the world is ruled by people who like shite music, you see, she said.

Our day will come, I said.

Both of us looked to the DJ as he shouted, And now the moment you've all been waiting for. PJ Burren, go home, because tonight, at Planet 2001, it's Skanky Malachy and The Skeletons!

The disco balls stopped rotating, and all the lights dimmed. The crowd yelled as smoke gushed out of a dry-ice machine on stage and there was this plinking sound of a tap dripping.

A green backlight flashed on and off in the smoke, and I caught sight of a skeleton at the drumkit, wearing a big grey wig and those glasses with springs on the frame so these cracked eyeballs boinged in and out.

He stood up off his stool, shook his drum sticks at us, leaned into the microphone.

And said Ha, Ha.

Which is when the soundman hit the echo switch.

Love yer optimism, said Siobhan.

I nodded, but I was also trying to sit closer to her by moving oh point five centimetres every ten seconds.

Devastating, i'nt it, I said.

Some women started screaming as three more skeletons marched through the crowd holding guitars, making talons out of their hands and snarling so people would jump out of their way. The skeletal drummer was tapping out a skiddleyup military beat like the stuff you heard on marches as the new skeletons mounted the stage, plugged their guitars in, and some backing track played howls and wind noises.

My thigh brushed against Siobhan's. Still, there was the Nazis, I said.

Who?

They were big into Beethoven.

A spotlight came on at the front of the stage and for the first time I noticed this black coffin with velvet trimmings.

A light fell on the coffin lid as it creaked open, and rising up out of it was Skanky Malachy, his face painted white, arms crossed over his chest.

Real slowly he rose, his eyes shut and star bursts painted on his eyelids, and real slowly he moved his head from side to side, looking all haughty and cold on us like some member of the undead asking himself, Who troubles my sleep of death?

Then he gazed with reddened burning eyes at some woman in the audience who was biting her knuckle. She gave out a yelp and drew back.

I said, As Berlin fell, they were chewing on cyanide, shooting themselves and listening to the Fifth Symphony. Does that mean Beethoven's shite?

Means we're fucked, said Siobhan.

A skeleton stepped over the guitar leads and held out a microphone while Skanky Malachy with his black nails extracted himself from out of the coffin.

He took the microphone, held it up to the light as if he'd just received a goblet of virgin's blood.

Who has proffered me this? he seemed to say, trying to work out what possible use it might have and he must have bitten some capsule, because blood was dribbling out of his mouth.

Then he laughed, low and deep laughter as if we were all in his dominion now.

There'll be bats next, said Siobhan.

Is there anybody here from Belfast? uttered Skanky, looking about.

Some girls raised their hands and squealed.

You are in my power ha ha.

The plinking sound of a tap dripping got louder as Skanky said, Anybody here from Derry?

A roar came up from a group of lads by the front of the stage.

You are in my power ha ha, said Skanky.

The lights went up. A skeleton struck a power chord.

1690, screamed Skanky, was the Battle of... the Groin!

Oh for fuck's sake, said Siobhan.

My sentiments exactly but the crowd exploded despite. The next thing Skanky was yelling, Dundrug, are you feeling alright, and when the crowd said, Yes, he even replied, I can't hear you.

But then, as though Skanky had been listening in to our musings all this time, this miracle occurred cos all of a sudden he yelled –

Mommy in a coma and Daddy on crack!

Crolly Doll Massacres by Fractured Jehovah!

And so without even thinking I grabbed Siobhan's hand and led her to the dance floor, where we started jerking round completely arrhythmic only I bumped straight into a man behind me who turned around and said, You fucking freak.

Then he swung back round and recommenced jumping up and down on his tiptoes.

After that, the Skanky show went down the toilets, so I moved back to the bar for another pint. I bought Siobhan a Pernod and black and asked for a shot of vodka in Eileen's orange juice. Teabags was standing at the bar holding his pint glass to his lips and looking shiftily left to right as though he'd got a first whiff of an evil conspiracy brewing. That's McHugh's woman thur, he said, out of the side of his mouth.

Not if I can help it, I declared, adding, did you see him?

I walked back to the table, dodging arms and legs like they were branches swinging back at you in a forest. I lowered the women's drinks dead centre with hovery moon landing precision cos I was terrified of a crash which would scupper my night of love.

Then I sat.

Siobhan crossed her right leg over her left in my direction which reminded me of a television programme I'd seen called *The Science of Body Language*. And exactly as Ma McHugh had mentioned the other night concerning the way women send out signals about their desire, she plucked a scrap of fluff off my shirt, and I wondered, could it be true, am I in?

And even though I'd kissed other girls before it was like the eternal question eating me up. My legs were trembling, and my brain was in a binary flash like the Hi Lo lights on the poker machine.

Eileen, however, had gone very quiet.

Eileen, said Siobhan. Is there something the matter?

Eileen stuck out her tongue. I'm fine, she said.

Are you sure? said Siobhan.

What are youse looking at me for? said Eileen.

Siobhan turned to me. My sister, she said.

Like a member of the Borgia family I watched Eileen drink her adulterated orange juice. Would she recognise the taste of vodka? I asked myself. Pushed up closer to Siobhan, I reflected that with several things happening at the same time, life at this moment was extremely vivid.

Suddenly McHugh appeared, standing over us with his pint.

How are you doing? he said.

I'm fine and yourself, I said, drinking.

For a second we all looked at each other and nobody talked.

Then the lights dimmed and Skanky said, Ration of Passion.

And the guitarist began playing the opening chords to Led Zep's Stairway to Heaven.

There's moments like this when you have to abandon your principles about what you dance to, and I calculated that I had about three minutes thirteen seconds to dance a slow before the song went into overdrive and the hard rock sequence began.

So I took her hand and there was no resistance as I walked once again with her onto the dance floor.

I put my arms around her waist and really normally she just put hers around my neck with a kind of a blush on her cheeks and her lips all tender swollen. Then she muttered something, and I answered by aiming my mouth for her ear and then suddenly towards her mouth, which was waiting for me with a touch of blackcurrant and tobacco inside.

I closed my eyes, pulled her closer and felt her heart going fast against me. Then it was like we drifted off, just drifted and sometimes dunted into other couples, then drifted off again into the sparkling blackness as though we'd slipped off the edge of the planet and were getting bounced along from one asteroid to the next.

At this moment I felt a tap on my shoulder. I opened my eyes and it was Mustapha Moran.

McHugh is after going up to the bar and ordering nine Pernods and black, he said.

Aye, right.

Looking none too happy either. Got a pound?

Why?

It's like I just need one more so I get a pint. What do you think of me hair?

He'd got it bleached since the day before so he looked like a ward of DJ Tingle in the nightmare of the future stakes.

Really great, I said, slipping him a pound.

Then I took Siobhan's hand again and led her to the lad with long grey hair who was sitting at the sound desk.

Does Skanky ever do a song called Fever? I said.

What, the one with the bass and clicking fingers? he said.

That's the one, I said, that's Fever.

No, he doesn't.

You don't do that song.

It's too old, and anyway, he's no soul.

I looked at the soundman standing in his booth in the shadows.

No soul at all, he grinned.

We returned to the table.

For some reason we both looked at Eileen. Her head was hanging.

Will you finish your orange juice, Eileen, said Siobhan.

Will you stop looking at me youse two, she slurred.

Her eyes were all bloodshot. Her cheeks shone and when

Siobhan tried to console her she completely broke down, saying there was nothing wrong with her, although I wondered whether it was the vodka.

McHugh walked past, holding five glasses of Pernod and black one inside the other. What with him drunk and Eileen broken-hearted, it was like being in a crisis centre.

Oh God, said Siobhan, he's in a state.

It's true you can't quantify passion. No Richter scales to plot it and no clocks tick to time the perfect kiss but something delicate slipped and broke right there, because afterwards, something had gone out of the kisses. And I really needed to know what.

Can't you see the sister's crying, she said.

She's tired, I said.

It's all the stimulation, you know? Yours in particular.

Mine?

Don't worry about it. Yesterday she was in love with Finbar.

We didn't speak for a moment.

Going back to the hotel after, I said.

Siobhan said, Back to Tubberboghey, more like.

In a car, I said.

No, we're walking. Starting a new job Monday.

Doing what?

Arts centre. Interrogation finished is it?

As if things couldn't get worse the national anthem started. So everyone stood up. Soldiers are we, it goes. The soldiers of destiny. Due to the great dignity of it, the disco lights stopped rotating out of respect and only the drunkest remained in their seats with stupefied expressions like really old relatives who laugh at the joke five minutes too late. I put my arms around Siobhan but she just shrugged me off.

Just like the song, I want to stand alone, she said.

The soldiers of destiny... said the song.

And the aspirations of the Gaels...

Okay, I'd never really learned the words.

But as the song got into the final lap, with the verse about the blood of enemies, it was that moment in the evening where everyone did Victory V's with their fingers, Victory for The Boys, Victory for Irish unity via an armed struggle!

Teabags and Punch, Mustapha and McHugh, swaying slightly, with his two fingers in the air and two glasses of Pernod in the other hand.

And all of a sudden I got this sentimental twinge in the guts that I too could join the community of Victory V signs for The Boys.

Victory V signs for my country – Ireland!

So based on that reasoning, as the music crescendoed, I put my own two fingers in the air and I felt the skin over my skull contract because just then I heard –

Would you ever grow up.

It was Siobhan. She had her coat and Eileen stood beside her.

And then the song was gone.

The DJ said Goodbye folks and safe home to ye, and the PA amps buzzed. I followed after her as she pushed through the crowds, holding up her coat and handbag and there was a din which I realised was folks talking.

I don't need walking out, Mister Armchair General.

But I can walk you out.

You stay here, she said. We've a car waiting. General staff probably needs you to discuss whose round it is next.

Eileen didn't say anything but just stood off to the side of us looking at me like she'd lost her illusions and had earned the insight that I was a total bollocks.

Siobhan leaned forward, pecked me on the mouth. She was wearing her Palestine scarf again.

Never mind, she said.

I walked back into the disco.

McHugh was sitting on a seat by himself while the barmen moved around him like rescue workers picking over an accident. He sat in the middle of the real lights, his eyes a fraction off from all the drink and the bouncers walking up to people saying, Come on now it's time to go home.

I sat down.

Give us that, I said.

The Astrud Gilberto moment, he said, handing me the glass.

I took a sip of Pernod.

The what?

McHugh slugged on his glass of Pernod and black. We looked ahead of us into the disco transformed in the real light, at the tables covered in ashes and the seats wet from spilt beer. The thin carpets sprinkled with butts.

There's a sound in the ear after you've been listening to loud music a long time. A ringing noise, a buzz as of television in empty rooms when transmission's ended. It feels like the end of the world sometimes, sitting there looking ahead, the music gone but buzzing in the ears, looking ahead because you think if you stare long enough something else might happen.

Come on lads, said the bouncer. Get out.

4.

Main Street Dundrug, and middle aged farmers' wives in summer frocks coming out of PJ Burren's concert were checking out mini-skirted Northern Ireland girls like they hailed from some other species of anthropoid.

And everybody was going for chips.

Despite this new entente between the generations Punch was scrapping in the Planet 2001 car park with some bogman from Ballybobeg. All I saw was Punch fall, get a kick in the head and then by some miracle jump to his feet and assume a stance like Bruce Lee.

Mustapha and Teabags stood behind him eating chips out of a plastic carton, licking curry sauce off their fingers not knowing whether to choose between the chips or the fight when a nun walked up to them and said, Cease this violence instantly!

And the boys stood around like they'd got their sums wrong.

Up the road McHugh ran at some seagulls picking through a half-eaten hamburger.

Quack, quack, you whores, he said.

And when he turned around his eyes were red, bloodshot.

Nothing doing, so we headed home along the sea front, behind couples making for the cliffs.

The Astrud Gilberto moment, said McHugh and I waited for him to qualify this with something like sanity but he stopped suddenly.

What, I said.

He pointed at two men outside his house who were picking at his Ma's potted plants on the window ledge. They held them up like cup final trophies.

Those are Ma's plants! said McHugh.

One man was short. He wore a scraggy blonde moustache that dropped down the sides Viking style while the other who now flapped his arms up and down as though attempting to fly in spite of the pot of flowers on his head was terrifyingly large and had a dense beard which seemed to grow even around the region of his eyes.

Hopping and stepping as they went, they both sang a song.

Up yer hole, up yer hole, up yer hole

And then,

Up yer hole, up yer hole, up yer ho-oh-ole

It was at this point that McHugh said, Are you ready?

It took me a while to understand him. Ready for what, precisely? I asked.

They've got Ma's plants, he said. And no one gets away with that.

The men had seen us, and were staggering our way as if they wanted to share their botanical discoveries.

Gets away with her plants? I said.

By now the men were just reeling past.

McHugh stopped the big man. What the fuck do you think you're doing with my plants? he said.

The big man grunted, swung his enormous fist and caught McHugh on the side of the head and he fell without a sound. It was really like one of those stories you hear about a tourist taking photos of a grizzly bear eating honey and then knocking the tourist's head clean off because it's just a bit annoyed.

Then the men were looking at me.

Hallo lads, I said.

The small man with the drooping moustache said, What's your fucking problem.

Before I could answer, I'm fine, I saw him raise the pot in

the air and I closed my eyes. There was a flash of light.

When I opened my eyes I was sitting on the ground, lumps of soil in my mouth and spilling from my hair. McHugh had vanished.

Above me, the men peered like surgeons over a patient.

Only a plastic pot, you fucking cunt, said the big man, pulling me up by the shirt.

Back on my feet again, I thought it was over. Then I saw his forehead come at me as the smaller partner aimed a well-spotted free kick into my shin. I threw up my elbow and the bristling head thunked against it, but I was too late to stop small man catch me straight on the side of the face. I staggered again, wondering when they'd get tired of the efficiency of it, but they just kept coming forward and I kept backing out into the road when it suddenly occurred to me that I ought to start running.

So I turned and started to run like fuck, and as I cut round the corner of The Chemist and up Barry Walsh's lane, the gravel blurring beneath me, a beer glass burst against the wall by my head. Another exploded on the ground before me. I jumped over the gate and hurtled round the back of the house, leapt a wall and landed on the old Koonlagh road.

After about two hundred yards I wondered if I ought to stop, cos the way I was running I'd be in Tievebawn mountain with the sheep before sun up. I turned round and then realised I'd shot straight past McHugh who was sitting on Gillan's stone wall.

Gillan's wall had been put together several hundred years ago without cement or mortar. It leaned against the angle of the hill and enclosed a field with a cottage in ruins, where the soil was clay and the three cows had cropped all the grass leaving only the rushes and ragwort. They were standing by the wall where McHugh sat, only when I walked back they slowly started to move away.

Are you in a hurry or something? he said.

I stopped and looked up the lane. It was empty. All I could hear was my panting, the patient tread of the cattle moving to a place of greater security and that distant roar of the sea which was in our ears all the time except we never heard it. I squinted into the dark, wondering when the men would suddenly come looming out of it but it was only stones, road and wind out there.

Sit down, said McHugh. You're making me nervous.

I sat down and kept my eyes on the lane. Out of the corner of my eye I saw the cattle looking at us. The wire along the edge of the wall had tufts of their hair caught in the barbs.

Followed you up the way. You were running a marathon or something.

That was really clever, I said.

What are you talking about? said McHugh.

Your shrubs.

They're my Ma's. And no one gets—

I gave McHugh a push. This guy just tried to remove my head like! I yelled.

McHugh pulled on his cigarette and he was smiling.

Will I tell you something, he said.

I was shaking from head to toe. I don't care, I said.

Suit yourself.

Whatever you're saying is no use to me.

Fine then, said McHugh.

He pulled on his cigarette.

After a while I said, They're only plastic fucking pots!

I could hear the paper burning on McHugh's cigarette. The cattle breathed and snorted in the dark and I got their damp methane whiff mixed up with the pollen that was released as they tore at the grass in tufts.

Those were The Boys, he said.

How do you know?

Man had a Long Kesh tattoo on his arm. But you just know anyway. Need to let off steam now and then.

Cause they've nothing better to do.

They've loads of things to do, boy, said McHugh.

Aye, plant bombs, shoot Brits, unite Ireland and beat up some teenagers. Hooray. We're in good hands. I can sleep sound now.

Stop ranting – do you want to know something?

No.

The brother's with them. Swear you'll say nothing.

I didn't speak.

Are you satisfied now? he said.

Is he good with the potted plants or something?

McHugh offered me a cigarette.

Do you realise we've scrapped with The Boys and we're still standing? he said. Like that's nothing to be ashamed of.

I began to laugh a bit, despite having received six punches and thrown precisely none.

I took his cigarette and put it in my mouth without smoking it. Weird things these fags, I said.

They help you breathe sometimes, said McHugh.

We compared wounds. McHugh had a scrape on the side of his head while there was lump about my jaw as though I'd been injected for a filling.

I dodged a headbutt though! I said.

Impressive, said McHugh. Did you see me swing at your man?

Not really.

That's your adrenalin, you go blind, like. Got them wirecutters?

I'd forgotten about them. They'd even got past the frisk at the entrance to the club.

I reached into my secret pocket and pulled them out. What are you planning on doing? I said.

A bit of rural regeneration.

He got up, and close to the edge of the posts snipped the barbed wire running above the wall. Then he leaped over the wall, loosened the posts, tugged them and flung them onto the road.

So you're the Dundrug saboteur?

Yep.

You're fucking mental.

No, I'm not. It's a project.

Can we go now?

Not until you look at the field.

I stood and looked at it a second. Minus the wire the cows could get over the wall no sweat, though by the way they were standing huddled near the ruined cottage they so far hadn't quite worked this out.

And? I said.

It's freed up so it is. But maybe you wouldn't understand. You being a Saxon and all.

I'm no Saxon. It's just where I was born.

So look at the field.

Yep. Totally freed up you fucking mentaller.

You're some poet.

McHugh turned back down the lane and I listened to the night sounds of birds letting out the odd cheep in this bush or that wind-blown excuse for a tree. It was really weird how about hundred yards out of Dundrug you were in the middle of real night with insect life and animals as though in a jungle only ever half tame.

Then we were back in Ballybobeg Road surprising some gulls who, now masters of the night, were walking about with their wings by their sides picking at dropped chip packets. All was the rustling of paper and screeches as they fought over the food and it hit me that they'd never tweet or cheep cause the sea isn't civilised either.

We could see the men staggering towards the town, kicking up chip papers and clouds of gulls.

The night was definitely over but as we got back to McHugh's house above The Chemist I noticed an orange light flickering on and off inside Pa McHugh's car, which was parked in front.

We moved closer.

McHugh said, Oh Jesus fuck.

Old Man McHugh had a navy blue Mercedes. One day he offered to give me a lift the way elders do here when they see you out enjoying a walk and the fresh air. He said he was going out my way. After that, he went completely silent as we drove up the new road. I settled into the bright quilted leather seat and the engine made a low expensive hum sound over the road, so smooth I couldn't even feel the road anymore, the Merc's long bonnet holding it all against the rolling fields, the tarmac a blur.

Right now that same car was looking none too invulnerable as the orange light went bright and the windscreen snapped. A tiny gush of smoke came out of the crack in the windscreen and suddenly there came a low droning fire buzz in the air.

All I could do was gawk at it with all the fire heat on just one side of my face.

The bonnet began to smoke and as though he were in a film McHugh said, She's gonna blow.

We ran out into the road and stopped and waited but the bonnet just continued to smoke.

Then there was a thump and the fire shot right through the car and black stinking smoke rose into the sky.

Do we know who did it? he said. Do we?

Before I could answer he said, It's the husband of the skull arse woman, fucking brilliant, and he ran to the door of The Chemist and started banging on it.

I stood in the middle of the road tranced by the flames and the flames' shadows rising up the height of The Chemist.

McHugh's parents came out into the street. His father did not say a word and his expression was the same as ever. If Krakatoa had just erupted or we'd been captured by a wandering herd of yeti his glasses would still have reflected the light and his beard would have just stood still.

Ma McHugh was in a Japanese kimono, her arms folded and she said, Who did this?

McHugh said, On the way home we just saw the car on fire, Ma.

She looked at me.

Saw no one, I shrugged.

Mister McHugh said, No use crying over spilt milk.

We watched the car burn, fill the street with a red glow which lit every house and wall and threw giant shadows of us down the road like some ridiculous Hollywood film with helicopters.

I noticed McHugh standing between his folks.

When the milk's spilt, said Old Man McHugh, then it's spilt. There's no use crying over it.

Ma McHugh pulled her pack of Rothmans Extra out of her kimono pocket and I noticed her hands were trembling.

That's the stupidest expression I've ever heard in my life, Tom, she said.

She lit a cigarette.

Cos there's seas of the stuff in this fecking world.

And it was then that the first bellowing cow appeared from Barry Walsh's lane and started bowling along towards Main Street.

Is that Barry Walsh's heifer? said Pa McHugh, pointing.

I watched as cow number two appeared.

This is your fault, said Ma McHugh.

I turned around. She was pointing her Rothmans Extra my way.

5.

It was five o'clock when I got home. And there was plenty of milk everywhere, not spilt – but somehow poured. The light was a sort of sparkling milkiness poured across the surface of the sea and spreading out enveloping everything. A milk mist hung above the grass tops and over the road all the way to the mountain. From the sycamore in the front garden a couple of birds cheeped and parped milkily and I thought everything would turn out fine until I saw the ladder standing up against the back wall reminding me how this had begun.

I gripped the sides and climbed one rung then another and the bathroom window was there open as if I were stepping into the jaws of a hangover. Or a bad dream.

I crept down the stairs in the hushed house and there in the bedroom on my bunk was a note from the world to come.

Folks discovered your plot to escape, your football head too ridiculous, sorry – Niamh.

I put my real head in my hands and closed my eyes.

I saw again Ma McHugh accusing me of releasing the cattle cos I was a godless Communist.

Then I saw Pa McHugh's car aflame with bits of glass falling to the ground and huge bubbles of melting leather popping and fuming.

Then I saw the man with the sticks going past us not even looking at the hell fire flames.

It was as if I had this experimental French film going on behind my eyelids, punctuated by the wee ones' snores, and the odd commentary from sleeping Niamh in one of those dream languages which was of no linguistic category known to man.

At nine I gave up and slunk into the kitchen. Plastic streamers hid us from the guests eating breakfast in the dining room. Da had a mug of tea in his hand and toast in the other, deciding which to go for.

I heard Ma behind the streamers chatting to the guests. Everything fine?

Oh lovely, they said. Just lovely.

Enjoy the PJ Burren concert?

Beautiful.

Just beautiful. He's a lovely voice.

Ma passed through the streamers and the smile on her mouth disappeared like a door closing.

Here's an apparition, she said.

Da sipped some tea and said, That's no apparition, that's a miracle.

I sat down. My head ached. So did my jaw which was feeling swollen up, still hot from the small man's slap.

Got a toothache? said Da.

No.

So what's in your mouth.

Nothing.

Depressed about the Jogger boy?

About who?

That singer, what's his name, the Zoltan fellow.

And what about him?

Ma sat down opposite me so I was facing them both as if I was up in front of a pair of social workers.

Shot himself on stage, said Da. Or no, he was going to shoot himself on stage, he was holding a gun to his head, and then some kid stepped up on stage with a gun himself and offered to shoot him. All the kids were yelling, No Jogger, don't kill yerself, but this lad grabbed the microphone and said, Jogger, do it, do it, for us. So yer man Jogger says, Right On, pressed the trigger on his own gun, and out of the barrel pops a wee banner that says Peace.

So is Jugger Zoltan dead or are you making this up to prolong the agony?

Nope, the kid blew his own brains out.

I said, It was to see a girl.

Strange times we be living in, said Da, looking at the semi circle his mouth had chomped out of the toast.

Still, he sighed, rock and roll never dies.

I held up a bit of toast and tried to force it into my mouth.

Da said, It's like I sometimes look at the Rolling Stones, them boys being about my age. They look a bit razzled, do Keith and Mick. Same generation but. Me fixing machines, them jumping up and down on stage.

Ma lifted up the pot. Are you going to get to the point? she said.

Da put his tea down. Sometimes I wonder whether they've had more fun than me, but no, I don't mind, I fix machines so that ye have all the fun. Incidentally, did *you* have fun last night?

Sort of, I said. Not exactly. Something else happened. Something serious.

Da raised the mug to his mouth and over the lip of it I caught his eyes looking frightened in a way I'd never seen them.

Surprise me, he said.

Ma came back with a full teapot and said, When we saw the ladder we thought it was thieves. Your Da went up to the bathroom with a hurling stick.

I took a deep breath and said, On the way home, we scrapped with two men and they set fire to Mr McHugh's car.

My head ached to say this.

Well good man yourself, said Da. That's brilliant. Congratulations.

Ma switched her smile back on but her eyes were a bit glazed as she hit the streamers with rashers and eggs for the PJ Burren fans, one of whom said, He had the home crowd wild singing My Darling from Dundrug.

A bit quickly Ma said, Do you need some brown sauce for that?

How much did you have to drink? said Da.

I extracted from my mouth the bit of mashed up toast I was trying unsuccessfully to chew without feeling half my head clang and in a really solemn voice said, Just a pint, and minding our own business. They just jumped us.

When Ma came into the kitchen she turned on the radio as though the news had gone national.

You're a smart man, said Da. You're some smart man. Do you know who it was?

From the North, I suppose.

They have anything to do with the McHughs?

What's that supposed to mean?

Da gave Ma a quick glance. And what about the guards, he said. You talk to them?

87

After, we didn't exactly see the lads do the car. So we said nothing.

There was like some mystery vibe coming off the pair of them as Ma opened the oven and brought out bacon and sausages. She laid them steaming in front of us.

Da said, If Lucky here isn't having some bacon, then I am.

A woman on the radio said, And I really trusted him, Pat.

Da came back from work in the afternoon. The wee ones ran from the swing he had set up under the tree. They ran and leaped onto the doorstep and when he got out of his car they pulled at his hand to see if he had anything in them, apart from his newspaper *The Dundrug Observer*.

Daddy daddy, they said.

He put his large set of keys on the kitchen table and put the newspaper beside it. Ma was battering the potato masher against the sides of the saucepan. She stirred the mash again, looking at him for news from the outside world.

I'd spent the entire day indoors watching TV as it replayed images of a kid called Earl Dyer blowing his brains out on a stage in Cincinatti while Jugger Zoltan waved a Peace sign at him and muttered something like, Awesome.

In the press conference afterwards Jugger Zoltan kept saying his show was not about death.

My show is a representation of death, he said. It's a wind up, it's a joke.

His voice was sort of flat like a professor, an effect somewhat undermined by his incisors filed down so they looked like fangs. And there were kids doing a vigil outside the kid Earl's place, waving banners saying, Thank You Earl You Died For Us.

And a California chick was saying to the cameras, Thank you

Earl. Only you are Real.

And I wondered whether to be real you had to die. Cos it seemed like a drastic solution somewhat.

But the other devastating experience of the night before was playing about in my head, and by that I am not referring to the scrap.

It was as if the first kiss of the night before had triggered something in me, like, as WB said, a fire in my head.

For instance, in front of the mirror, I'd said Her name a hundred times.

And there was still her perfume in my clothes, so I smelled them.

Da pulled up a chair and sat down.

You in the habit of setting cows free? he said.

No.

Well that's already something.

And what about the other lads, said Ma.

Guards didn't find them anyway, said Da.

Did anyone else?

Ah now, said Da, and he picked up his newspaper.

Ma gave him a look and went back to the sink. I suppose the car's insured anyway, she said.

Oh aye, car's insured alright. Happy about that, hard man?

I didn't say anything.

Yessir, said Da. No one messes with Tom McHugh's car, if you know what I mean. Do you know what I mean?

What are you saying? I said.

I don't know. You've been living here the same length of time as me. Things get settled Dundrug style. What do they call it – correction of anti social elements?

My little sisters slipped onto Da's lap and he bounced them

up and down and let them slip off his knee but saved them at the last minute.

I smelled my teeshirt for the five hundredth time and I was about to say something when he put his fingers to his lips.

The kids laughed, helplessly.

Then Niamh walked in.

It's Granny, she said.

What about her?

Exactly, I don't know, she said. She just said she was going for a walk.

Part 3

1.

I was on a seven o'clock curfew until the end of the holidays, so as far as the evening danders were concerned, my summer was over. Plus, I didn't see anything of McHugh. Whenever I called down to The Chemist of an afternoon Ma McHugh'd come swishing out through the streamers and say, Well if it ain't Jerome Maguire the godless Communist.

Any chance of Finbar coming out?

Finbar's studying praise the Lord and what about yerself and yer life of Philosophy?

The smile was there, but it looked like something that required surgery to get rid of. The silveriness and bounce were still authentic, but the shutters were closed down. From being my best forty-year-old friend, she'd suddenly taken a dislike to me. I didn't quite understand why she blamed the burning car on me, but that seemed to be her drift.

But beyond storming The Chemist, there was no way past her.

I shrugged, and sloped off, and even when I attempted calling his mobile it was off.

Instead, I did a tour round the amusement arcade, where the poker machines had gone all stubborn on me, and to cap off my Dundrug promenade I'd walk past the Stella Maris Hotel, even though I knew Siobhan wasn't there.

As for Philosophy, there were no such books selling in these parts, so up on the cliffs I would sit watching the waves crash on the rocks, and wonder why the backs of them looked so smooth and oily with delicate white filaments running through them like combed hair.

And I tried to work out, Why me?

Which is to say, why was it Jerome Maguire and not, like, DJ Tingle gazing out this pair of eyes, operating these hands, living inside this body? Indeed, why weren't I a Laplander tracking elk in the snows or some girl called Sayuri dancing in a strip joint in the bay of Tokyo? Could I always hold onto to my me-ness, and if not, could I slip into McHugh's mind, or introduce myself into a goat, or have a cat's dreams, if I found the right equation or something?

What made me me?

And like, why now? Why hadn't I been born in the year 3058, when the world would be one peaceful federation and have trade relations with beings from the Fourth Dimension?

But in answer to all this, the only image that slipped into my mind's eye was the ABBA women singing Dancing Queen, Dancing Queen...

In the crushing meantime, in between these idle speculations amidst the cattle and the sea, I had to do community service and keep an eye on Granny's movements.

No idea how she did it, but on the day of her disappearance she went ten miles out to Dunfagart and we reckoned she must have walked it.

Some neighbours tipped Da off about her pushing in the door of her old cottage and refusing to come out. When we drove out there an hour later, along with Aunt Kathleen who was over from London, Granny was sitting on a chair in the old kitchen, and Kathleen started weeping cos all this reminded her of how poor as shit the Maguires used to be, though now she lived in Greenwich with this English builder called Derek who had a wooden leg.

It was round about dusk so there were feeding swallows veering and then doing wee back flips into nests woven in the collapsed thatch, and amidst all that twittering Granny mistook Da for her father, gave out to him for coming back drunk from market again. She even started yelling at me cos I slipped into a room where a black wireless stood on a wooden chest cos apparently there was a ghost lurking.

Have the gardai come? she said. Cos I'm not leaving here. And I'm not signing nothing either.

We drove back down the mountain lanes with Aunt Kathleen weeping in the car and I felt somewhat wan too. The Granny situation didn't look too good, and it had me well scared, but most of the time my brain kept switching back over to Channel Siobhan and everything else didn't seem that relevant to me.

But in the week that followed I still sloped around after my grandmother, taking her up the cliffs, sitting in the wild field, watching cricket on BBC Ulster and trying to work out the rules.

And not even correcting her when she called me Michael. She told me about the time I'd wrestled a bull to the ground, how I could drink thirty pints in one sitting, and how I'd carried weapons for The Boys during the civil war.

Aye, I'd say, and I'd wonder if she'd detected in me this wild inarticulate streak, that I'd end up expressing my darkest passions in bottles of hard liquor and the dance floors would be strewn with the crumpled heaps of lads whose heads I'd clunked together.

That seemed pretty cool, sometimes.

Also, she told me that back in the thirties spirit women used to visit the dance halls recognisable cos of their stunning beauty and the way they floated along the ground. If you looked down, you'd see their feet were back to front, but by then you'd be lost and kidnapped off to hell.

But apparently I had kissed one and survived.

That cloud looks like the devil, she'd say, pointing at a cumulus stand above Tievebawn.

And I'd go, That's right.

We'd be right there in the field as tractors came hurtling out of the country lanes with big black bags of silage leaking the stink of stewed apples and I knew she was fading out into her spirit world.

And I knew that if I didn't want to go down with her, I'd have to start concentrating on the year ahead, my last year in Dundrug. I'd have to prepare for the glorious future.

In anticipation of which, the folks had given me my old room back ahead of season's end.

So I had my view on the mountain back, and I could follow the road and fields and the part where the fields rose and broke off like a great fracture and beyond it that wideness in the air which meant the sea.

I could read my books in this room I'd fitted out with a sort of Japanese aesthetic, of few possessions and low key lighting.

Though in the wardrobe folded up was the school uniform that for one more year I'd have to put on every morning from eight thirty till four.

Sometimes, I thought that final year ahead was going to go like a penance, that the skills of Dundrug's best and brightest teachers were sort of lost on me now, not cos I didn't want to learn. It was just that I wanted out.

But I knew I only had to go up to those cliffs and I'd be okay. If I looked at the mountain standing like a massive wave against the fields I'd be okay. I'd be okay another year cos I knew the place had worked into me deep.

I was Dundrugistani alright, with a bit of hardness and blackness and the sea detonating off inside.

On the day the curfew had lifted, I was looking at the fields turning brown from the rain and big puddles in them glittering like blue mirrors.

I'd been checking out an OS map to find the caves the German tourists were on about, but then I thought of writing a poem about this swan I'd seen gliding like a ship from the river into the flooded patch.

But all I could do was the following, ahem –

The children they are tall
Their limbs are cold and lean
Like swans they cannot walk
Like swans they are obscene

They dance in jerks and starts
Of economic graphs
And puke in tall new streets
Like dead new born giraffes

95

I was wondering what this had to do with Siobhan when it hit me that you could sing it to the melody of My Darling from Dundrug.

After that, I picked up a compass and scratched her name into the palm of my hand.

McHugh'd often said the best thing was to scratch a line along the wrist and stay up late one night drinking. The next day you had to pass the woman you adored and look as if you were dying from her. You had to make sure in a subtle way she caught sight of your falsely slashed wrist or else she'd think you'd just been drinking.

Women, he'd said, are impressed by souls in torment and mutilation to prove it.

The sister Niamh, however, had other theories.

Oh my God, you've gone psycho, she said.

I shrugged. I hadn't shaved my eyebrows off, nor taken a razor to my throat. It just seemed appropriate to have her name in the palm of my hand a while, cos I hadn't dug the compass point in too deep so the cuts would fade with time.

But as I read the shaky poem, I was wondering whether I hadn't gone a tad far.

Never mind, I thought, and walked into town.

To catch the march.

On Main Street, twenty bands were parading, lads in black berets, black sunglasses and green combat wear marching, piping on flutes, tin whistles, recorders, squeezing accordions, tapping snares.

And always some lad built like a sea-lion battering a bass drum.

July 12th was over, so now it was time to show the Orange lads across the border that we in terms of martial songs and stiff legged marching had material as crap as theirs.

Though you couldn't really say such stuff out loud.

Teabags Malone sat on a window ledge outside the Four Provinces Gift Shop, rubbing his huge conk, and looking at the snatter he'd just decorated the footpath with.

Beside him there was an old chalk mural of Bobby Sands, and beneath it was written – Bobby Sands, MP, Died so Ireland Can be Free.

The mural had been touched up so many times in the last decade the features had dissolved so you had to read the caption to know you weren't looking at Jesus Christ.

I bid Teabags Good Morrow, and asked if I could sit beside him.

As long as you don't start feeling me up, he goes.

I sat down. I said, Any sign of McHugh these days?

Would you English bastards go quiet as a mark of respect for the Republic, he said, pointing at a new band in black playing the same instruments and battering the same drums as the last group.

Aye fine, I said, and watched the band go past, the lanky, the squat, the brick shit houses all about my age but with a certain zeal politics-wise that I couldn't quite tune in to. Not for want of trying, like.

But no doubt about it, that three-beat marching sound had the hairs stand to attention at the back of yer head, and the bass drum got the blood a dancing, so I could understand what the Orangemen got so intoxicated about.

Makes you proud, don't it? said Teabags.

Makes you want to jump up and start scrapping, I said.

What in deepest fuck would you know about that?

Not much, but just stop calling me an English bastard.

Teabags looked me at with a start. So what manner of bastard are you?

It's just where I was born.

Aye that's all intellectual edifying and such, but you're different is all. Like another religion or something.

Thanks.

For instance do you believe in the Virgin birth?

Do you?

There you go, that's exactly yer problem, he said.

He rubbed his nose, moved his head from side to side and started whistling to himself as though playing the pipey two-tone hoot a Brazilian samba band makes.

Kind of fits, I said.

Nothing like yer Brazilian stuff to perk matters up, he said.

Then he said, Only the chances of a Brazilian chick sucking you off in this neck of the woods is kind of slight.

I made to go.

Come here, he said, let's go for a walk. I've done my bit for Ireland, like.

Whistling samba till the band music faded, we cut up the lane behind the amusements, went left along the sea front road till we were standing in front of the Stella Maris Hotel and all of a sudden through a cloud, the brunt of the sun was on us.

It was mixed up with heavy sea air, and carrying that squealing sound from the beach, of kids entering that alien element sea water, and wondering whether it was going to be good to them or not.

There was still a big banner proclaiming WELCOME HOME PJ hanging up in front of the Stella Maris, only someone had written in felt tip pen, You Bollocks, underneath.

That was Punch, said Teabags.

He pointed into the hotel reception area. Cop a look at that man, he said.

Mustapha Moran was standing behind the reception desk wearing a black suit and answering the phone. His hair was still an abominable blond but slicked back all tidy and clean.

That's what's happened to one of Dundrug's biggest street scrappers, said Teabags. Remember a month ago he kicked a man so hard in the nuts you could only see the whites of his eyes as they carried him off. Now he's got a wallet with a photo of a Lamborghini sports number inside, and he says he building up to that.

Why the change? I said.

Man was revolted by his life of violence, the sight of yer man coughing his testicles up. Decided to call it a day.

He shook his head. You get these lads, they're like hurricanes, he said. Only hurricane's got just the one idea. It blows like fuck a while, then it's all spent. Then it becomes a capitalist.

And what about you?

Going to London, I suppose.

To spend yerself amongst the English bastards?

He looked at his scuffed knuckles and said, You haven't a fucking clue, do you?

About what?

You know where McHugh is right now? Up in Dublin seeing a shrink.

We walked down to the beach shelter at the end of the road behind the amusements, looking at the outdoor pool that'd been closed twenty years, but which folks still called The Ha'Penny. We sat down beneath graffiti which said IRA and Johnno loves Tracey Belfast.

Teabags said, His folks had the guards come in and put a chemical in the till cause they were losing money all the time. When his hands came out in green. They didn't have a clue like.

99

They thought it was Punch or me doing it so that's why they were sleeping downstairs all the time. Have you got no fags?

I don't smoke, I said.

So there's like a beardy psychiatrist performing tests on him. Is it something to do with your Ma? they ask and then he has to identify these blobs and not say it looks like a bat cos they'll think he's psycho.

Are you joking me?

Swear to God. It's like the brother, you know.

What about him.

The brother went funny after he'd seen tinkers fighting in Main Street. Saw a man get a pike in his neck. Awful odd after that.

He was never in the North?

In the North? What for?

I just thought McHugh had some brother who was a snappy dresser like, I said.

Teabags pulled a cigarette out his pocket. McHugh made a big mistake refusing to tell the guards who burned the car, he said.

Why's that?

They were onto him about cutting the fences down. It was getting like Spain out there with them cattle running amok in case you didn't notice. Frankie Bullen and Barry Walsh were going nuts over it. Cops were prepared to give McHugh a chance cos of his Ma being posh. Less so because of the Da.

What about the Da?

Ah now you were born yesterday man. What about the Da?

You're saying the Da is someone, like?

I'm saying the Da was like someone. Once. In a parallel world, if you get my drift.

I looked up the street. Coming round the sea road to avoid

the march there was a truck from the slaughterhouse loaded with rotting offal.

Chip off the old block is McHugh, said Teabags.

How that?

The old man was freedom for Ireland. The son saves cattle.

As the truck passed we held our noses and watched as bits of offal slopped out onto the road.

Though that's where they're headed anyway, said Teabags, pointing at the truck.

I got up and waved at Teabags and it occurred to me then that he was about eight years older than the rest of us, like Punch Gilbride, and even if he went away he'd be back, cos he'd prefer having a reputation in Dundrug than being a nobody in London.

I went onto the Tubberboghey road and stuck my thumb out. Out of the drizzle an old Renault 5 pulled up with a priest at the wheel. A mini pine tree and a plastic Virgin swung off the rear view mirror.

Come on in! he said, not even checking out my wet clothes to ascertain the extent to which they might ruin the passenger seat.

Going to Tubberboghey, I said, taking care not to blurt out Father like a real Christian though it was on the tip of my tongue. He was a plump priest with wild bubbly hair and cheeks of cracked blood vessels like someone had taken a red pen to them. He pressed down hard on the accelerator and swung out from behind a bread van. We flew towards a lorry coming the other way and he said, Go on, baby, go on, giving the car a slap of encouragement on the steering wheel. I sank into the seat as he swung back into the left lane.

Good baby, good! he said. Then, looking at me all the time, he said – Saw the march?

I looked out at the road. If he wasn't going to look at it, someone had to. I could feel a blush come over me as I said, Yep.

Love it. Saying a decade of the Rosary so they were. For peace, like. Her name's Siobhan?

I closed my left hand. Excuse me? I said.

Many splendoured thing the old love business, what?

I squirmed yet again and he nearly drove into a ditch at a bend. Then we went first up then down a bridge under which a river trickled.

Notice anything? he said.

The bridge?

Have the fields turned pink?

I was driving with a psycho priest! Still green, I answered.

Still some dribble of grime running from the eaves of them bungalows out there?

I looked out of the side window. There's dribble right enough, I said.

Used to be the border checkpoint back there, he said. The old Irish army. A lad behind a sandbag with a machine-gun smoking a fag, not standing idly by, what? Every time I went over the checkpoint he hid the fag cause I'm a priest. So now you know. We're in British territory! Amazing, isn't it? Different laws, different ways, right?

You make an adjustment in your head, I offered.

Red post boxes! he said.

We were driving slowly through Killballen. I didn't say anything. Because it was a day of marches all over the province, the British soldiers had come out of the local garrison. They were checking out the street as a woman came out of the local Spar carrying two plastic bags. A Jack Russell walked behind her, his tongue lolling about as he sniffed the

102

air in front of the butcher's where a soldier was kneeling and sighting with his gun.

It all looked really normal, in fact. Just like the good old days before the Peace!

We were a couple of miles short of Tubberboghey. The priest said, Given up on God too, I suppose.

Don't believe in him at all.

The priest started laughing to himself. You don't believe in him? he said, and pulled over onto a lay-by by the lough. That's the funniest one I heard, I can tell you.

The rain swept across the fields and the lough in great flapping sheets.

The priest slapped the steering wheel.

That's the greatest cosmic bejaysus of a joke I ever heard, he said.

Siobhan was surprised.

I stood outside the Tubberboghey Arts Centre watching the employees file out. I was a wee bit out of breath, cos the priest's car had broken down and I'd run the last mile.

She pulled away from the group with a male about her age who had a streak of purple on his forelock.

You're wet, she said.

I am.

Looks like you must have walked it.

I would've walked it for you, I offered.

What?

It's easy getting a lift.

Meet Hugh, she said, a fellow employee.

Hugh had a cheerful abstracted look. How's life? he said.

It's fine, I replied.

Hugh's big into computers and has his own band, haven't you, Hugh.

Check, said Hugh, giving me a thumbs up.

Has his own studio too.

We must have loads in common, I said, shrugging.

But no one laughed, and as Siobhan walked past me Hugh held back beside her so I had to step off the kerb and walk in front. I turned to talk and when she replied she was looking at the footpath.

D'you fancy coming with us? she said.

We sat in the lounge of a pub.

What are you having, I said.

Tea.

Nothing stronger?

If you want a pint don't let me stop you.

I will.

It's good after exertions.

Hugh looked at her full of admiration.

I went up to the bar and ordered tea and a pint of lager. The barman said, How old are you.

Nearly eighteen.

Have you no ID.

Forgot it.

He poured me a pint and put it down hard on the counter and said nothing when I thanked him.

Got no sterling either, he said.

None. Just up for the day.

When I got back to the table they were looking at documents like perfect students, and when I put the drinks down they looked at my pint.

A wee bit early, said Hugh.

I closed my left hand with SIOBHAN cut into it, keeping it on my knee like something not entirely my own. I drank the beer and said, Been writing any poems?

Some, she said, following with her eyes the cloud of smoke that went drifting past my head.

I drank quickly. I could see Hugh think about all the smart things he would tell her afterwards and I envied him.

Which means I wanted to empty a gun into his kneecaps and skull.

Can I see some? I asked.

Oh they're not for the eyes of the world, she said.

I felt a curdling sensation in my guts. In proper conversations folks lay down a bridge for you to cross when speaking. Here, I felt like I was stepping out into a ninety foot chasm as I said, Any Emily Dickinson influence there?

Ah now.

I was in free fall alright, so I finished my pint. Then I stood up quickly and the blood flowed out of my head. I put out my hands to keep straight.

That must have been the walk, said Hugh.

I went to the toilets where I spotted a Durex machine with varieties like Fruit Flavours and Ribbed whose relevance in my life seemed to have vanished as I dried my hair under a hand dryer and sat on the toilet bowl in one of the cubicles wondering why this expedition wasn't going as brilliantly as anticipated.

Was there anything real going on here at all or was I truly psycho?

I walked back out to the lounge concentrating on each step I took in case I fell over, and I felt Siobhan's eyes on me as though I was entirely made out of glass and she could see all the cogs and springs inside me clunking and seizing up. She had put her cigarettes inside her coat. I sat down and picked up my glass and tried to drink from it despite the fact that it was empty.

Listen, I said.

I leaned towards her to create a confidential atmosphere which would exclude Hugh.

I wasn't thinking straight that night when I made the V sign, I said. I wasn't thinking because you know why.

What are you talking about, she said.

I just did the V sign because there wasn't much in my head at the time.

She frowned. Don't go dwelling on it too much, she said.

I'm not dwelling on it. I'm just telling you so you know.

Well now I know.

It was then Hugh muttered something, as though to himself, but it was loud enough –

Wake up baby the nineteenth century's dead, he said.

I turned to him. Excuse me?

Hugh looked past my head interrogatively. What's that? he said, into the distance.

You said something about the nineteenth century being dead.

Haven't you heard?

Siobhan was texting someone on her mobile. What are you suggesting? I said.

Dunno, said Hugh. Prozac, lithium, a good counsellor?

Don't quite get you, I said, but instinctively I clenched my hand so he couldn't see the scabs on it.

Didn't think you would.

Siobhan stood up. This is fun but I've got to go, she said. Night school beckons, the corridors of knowledge and all that.

After receiving a look from her Hugh jumped up.

He said, Hold the line we are trying to connect you.

Then he walked out the door.

Before I could ask of him further explanations as to his insights, Siobhan grabbed my arm.

Will you see me out? she said.

I stood out on the street with her. We were in Tubberboghey. I could see the soft sloping island bifurcate the river, and standing on it a castle carved out of granite.

I pointed at the Union Jack flapping off a pole.

I saw the Queen of England once, I said.

You did?

We were junior school kids. We got a tube down from Kilburn and they handed out little plastic Union Jacks. We stood in front of Buckingham Palace waving the flags as the limo went past. I saw her hand waving. And I yelled something at her.

And that was?

My Grandda had been spending time with us. Whenever he saw a Union Jack, he'd stick his tongue out the side of his mouth and do a kind of salute, and say, Up the Republic.

So that's what you said?

I thought it was being respectful, like.

We looked at the flag flapping on the pole.

Do you want me to tell you something? she said.

Then she took my hand marked out with cuts.

She leaned forward and kissed me on the mouth.

She put her lips to my ear.

And said, No.

Five minutes later I was trudging out on the wet road, a nineteenth century has been. I stuck out my thumb and an Audi pulled up. The driver said he was going a bit of the way.

We drove towards the Republic, through churned up black fields over which clouds of rooks hovered and dived. The driver had a whiff of aftershave coming off him and on one hairy wrist a gold watch stared. He looked thoughtfully out on the road, nodding, breathing out through his nose when I made the crushingly obvious statement that the weather was far from satisfactory.

It was while going through the forested lakelands that he asked whether a bit of music would offend me. I didn't understand a word he'd said. The only thing in my head was the image of Siobhan standing on the street in her native Tubberboghey.

So I surfaced.

Excuse me? I said.

Would you mind a bit of music?

Open to anything except PJ Burren.

Poor old PJ. You worry about him, do you?

Among other things.

You need to let it all flow, he said.

I was still stunned by his intervention when he hit the play button and a harpsichord and cello with voices rising around went up and up until it was all layered. It brought out good stuff about the lake, the forests and the rain you don't normally get from other sounds.

Although I tried to hold onto that one sharp image of Siobhan standing in the middle of the Tubberboghey street I couldn't. She just faded as the music started to dominate the landscape.

But as it crescendoed with a rumpty tum finale the driver clicked on the indicator, and veered to the side of the road where a lane pulled off into the heart of the country.

He said something before I left.

Look after your hand better the next time you cut it.

I began to walk.

The road was completely empty. My head buzzed with the music although I couldn't quite get the melody. As I walked through the forest with the sun a glare behind the clouds it passed through me though. It was like the trees and the earth and my mind were in some precise configuration and had gone click together as when the sun and moon line up and there's a glittering corona around the blackness. I heard the harpsichord grinding out star music above the road and even though dusk was coming on I didn't want to walk anymore. In case the sensation would leave me.

As the road ran along the lake shore I pulled the poems I'd planned to give Siobhan out of my secret pocket and read them again.

I shrugged, cos I knew that even an old sock of wind like WB Yeats had written a line as forever as –

Because a fire was in my head

So I made paper boats out of the poems, and launched them out onto the lake.

I watched them totter about in the waves when this big heavy bird the shape of a flying boat blew past them across the water a foot off the surface.

So the poems just gave up and sank.

Then I started walking again.

At a sharp turn in the road I saw a sign which said *Turn off your Headlamps before Mounting the Ramp*. In the middle of the empty road there was a traffic light on red making a soft buzzing noise and above it obscured by trees a machine gun turret.

At the end of the ramp I saw two men moving, their faces painted with black stripes, leaves spraying out of their helmets.

They had machine-guns.

All about the trees dripped. I looked around, back down the road where I'd come from. I no longer knew where I was. Then I heard a shout.

I turned. They had crouched down and were sighting down the barrels of their guns. Out of the black face-paint their eyes shone green. I pulled to a stop no longer knowing what to do with myself.

Don't move, one said.

He did something with his gun.

Where you going? he said, his accent a Cockney one.

I didn't know if I should answer or not.

Where are you going?

To the Republic.

Stand right there.

What are you doing on this road?

I put my hands up. I got a lift, I said. I got dropped off a mile back. I think I must have missed a turn. I didn't know you were here.

Well, surprise.

The second soldier said, What's wrong with your hand.

I opened up my left hand with SIOBHAN cut into it.

Never pick at scabs, he said. Might give you cancer.

Don't move your hands, said the first. You'll put them down when I fucking tell you to.

Don't stay in the middle of the road. Go there.

I walked to the verge.

And kneel.

Kneel?

Need some help with that?

The Cockney rose to his full height of about six foot eight all gangling and gigantic jaw and lit a cigarette as his littler partner trundled off into the camouflaged cabin to radio for instructions. He had a large nose shiny on the ridge like Teabags Malone and I wondered whether they didn't have a common ancestor before the separation of the two land masses.

He said, Do you like Frank Sinatra songs?

The damp was seeping into my knees. Far off, some cattle bellowed and a tractor ran down a lane.

Sometimes, I said.

What do you mean sometimes.

There are some I like, others I don't.

D'you like the song called Clouds?

Don't know it.

Course you know it. Everyone does. Your parents know it, so you know it. Everything that's happened these last forty years is in your head.

But I don't know it.

The gangling soldier said, Listen, it goes –

Ice cream castles in the sun,

The moon the stars for everyone. Do you know it?

I think I heard it once. Are them the right words?

There you go. I really love singing that song when I'm on the Irish road with my gun and watching people. Great song.

It's a charming song, I said.

And most particularly I love singing it to people when I stamp on their heads.

I swallowed and looked at the cabin, which contained the Small soldier, who, in stark contrast to Gangling Cockney Psycho, might turn out to be a friend, if only we could get acquainted.

It really gives me a buzz that, said Gangley, pulling on the cigarette as at some fond memory. Stamping people's heads in.

111

Legally, I mean. Cos when you stamp on people you get to know about them a lot. As the blood comes out their ears.

I'm London born too, I said.

He looked at his cigarette and tapped some ash off it. You London what?

I don't know.

You said you're London born?

Not at all.

So what the fuck were you saying?

I was wondering if Frank Sinatra had ever sung in London.

Jesus Christ he's retarded, said Gangley, tisking.

I saw a car drive over the ramp with the driver looking out at me with my hands upon my head since they'd been getting tired hanging up in the air and the lads hadn't noticed. He went up and over the ramp and his car engine switched off. The tall soldier flicked his cigarette away and crouched down at the window.

The Frank Sinatra song began to turn in my head.

The driver said, Need a lift?

With my hands on my head I said a lift would be fine.

The man looked at the two British soldiers.

Right there, lads, he said.

The tall soldier said, I never believed in Clouds, at all.

What? I said.

Forget it, he said.

The driver released the clutch and pulled out. What the hell were you doing at the checkpoint? he asked.

I'd forgotten about it, I said.

You wouldn't need to be absent-minded about it too much, hi.

Maybe not, I said.

But it was while we were crossing into the Republic that I told him there was something about the guns that I just couldn't believe. It might have been that the soldiers' faces were painted and the leaves splaying out of them but I just kept thinking the guns weren't real. They were a game.

The driver pushed his car into a lower gear as he slowed into Ballybobeg.

I can tell you for a fact that they're real, hi.

He pulled the car to a stop by the bridge.

And no mistake about it, he added.

2.

I was getting more and more stumped about war. Its causes got even more mysterious. There were the ones at school, the world square and flat, and territories drawn upon it. Red counters to the east, blue counters to the west. The dice fell. It was a game of Risk. I picked up the dice. I looked across the table at McHugh.

Say your prayers, I said. Because when I'm president of the world federation there'll be none of that.

It was one of the last times I saw McHugh. I'd been walking home when I spied the light on in the third parlour. For old times' sake I tossed a stone at it. A minute later he was standing at the front door, his finger over his lips.

And I discovered Siobhan sitting in the parlour at the Risk board. My heart started thundering in my chest. I wasn't over our story, but I tried. I gave her a smile like I was chewing on something gone off.

I threw the dice. McHugh's armies fell.

Why are you red? she said.

Like I ought to be an emerald green or something?

I threw the dice. She never saw my hand, nor the poems. I

controlled Alaska, Canada, drove through the Americas until my armies touched two oceans. I'd wasted a hundred red counters, all that parody of slaughter with a single idea in my head. They had fallen and I kept moving.

It was Siobhan's turn.

South-East Asia, she said.

What about our truce?

Truce whatever, she said. I'm attacking you now.

She had massed armies turn after turn in Indonesia. So she swept through me. I watched Siberia fall.

Alaska, she said.

I said nothing. She stopped at the borders of Brazil, her armies spilling over into the ocean. Then McHugh hit me in Newfoundland, moved down the east coast. I was cooked, alright, with one last button holding onto Brazil.

I said to myself it was not an army but just a man who'd thrown his gun away so I moved him away from the smoke and blood of battle to Rio, to a beach with a highway, skyscrapers, and jungle behind going into a continent so enormous he'd never get his head around it.

I picked up the dice.

McHugh said, There you go – it's that Astrud Gilberto moment.

You're always saying that.

Aye, well that's what it is.

He didn't say a word for a minute, then:

You know the song, the one about Ipanema? It means you got one song, but the person it's aimed at isn't listening.

He blushed deeply. Then he said, It just hit me like that.

I threw the dice and said, You mean that soppy song.

It's not soppy. It's romantic.

Well thanks very much, hi.

Not everything's about you, you know.

Which was when Ma McHugh came in.

Ah Jerome it's yourself.

Naw it's his dark side clone, said McHugh.

Still got yer Padre Pio card? she said.

Yep, I said, though I'd given it away weeks before.

You know he was bi-locational, she said.

Stop talking filth, Ma.

Bi-locational I said. So he could be in two places at the one time.

You're still talking filth.

So keep praying, she said, clapping her hands, cos you never know!

Then she leaned over Siobhan and said, Isn't that right sweetheart.

Siobhan said, I'm not here, Mrs McHugh.

And she was right, cos she wasn't there. At that moment she vanished.

I mean that she weren't even there that night. I mean I wished she had been. I just kept thinking she would be in the room.

But after Tubberboghey I never saw her again.

Then Ma McHugh, who was real enough, laughed, gave my spikes a wee tug and walked out, leaving a cloud of smoke behind her.

And I wondered what kind of Fever had possessed her once to opt for a man like Pa McHugh, if everything Teabags'd said about Pa McHugh was correct.

Indeed, I wondered what Fever possessed anyone.

I didn't know about war and its causes but I knew about love.

Sort of.

I knew certain varieties of it. And maybe not the real one.

I walked back home that night and filled the rubber with water until it burst. Others had done it before me. The black woman had thought love was a fever before me.

Though I wasn't going to be bitter. I mean you can be bitter, but not like milk gone off.

But like a lemon bitter. That's okay.

McHugh and the family packed up and disappeared that Christmas. The Chemist and the flats across the street were up for sale and they drove off in a brand new Hiace van. Back to Belfast.

They left with their mysteries intact.

Life was a little quieter. I finished reading *King Lear* that I'd started on that summer. Kent refuses to take part in the new law of the land. That's for the weaker Albany. There's Edgar too. But you're not sure of them. It just peters out on a strange note. You're sure of nothing and you always keep rooting that it resolves itself and then it just doesn't.

You keep thinking that everything resolves itself neatly like in a tale and it just doesn't. A tale, a story, your very own story. The only one. And it doesn't.

I was up on top of Tievebawn mountain with McHugh before he left. We'd found the cave, but the only Neolithic painting we saw inside was something done in Tippex that said, Teabags Malone Was Here.

McHugh sat down on a rock and lit up and said, Would you look at that light.

I looked with him.

There was a grove nearby planted with mountain ash. The

trunks were knotted, whorled, they'd stood the wind for centuries. The branches wobbled like upside down legs. About the rocks – the whins, and a wren that flips out of one, and the twigs quivering in its wake.

We were poring over the patterned fields as they shelved off to our very own Atlantic, mountains affording such Risk-board-like perspectives, towns to conquer, roads to set out on. We sat like gods plotting our next moves.

If I may be so bold.

I rooted in my pocket, pulled out a lighter and snapped it on. I watched the flame tremble and lean sideways, battered by the wind awhile.

The clouds were cruising above us like a flock of spaceships and the colours kept changing. Everything kept changing.

I looked at McHugh and I said there were more than that light.

I said there was music. It didn't have to be melodic.

We walked back to the road looking ahead of us. It was out there.

Thanks

To Jasmine Donahaye, my editor, for her queries, encouragements, hints, shouts, and to Richard Davies, the man from Neath who say yes.

To those patrons of the arts, willing or sort of drafted in, whose assistance meant the book could land, particularly Anne-Lise, and also Eve Carpentier.

Fever was sometimes written in other people's houses, so I thank them. The house at Ponceau, Maine et Loire, the house on Calle Fredes, Xert.

Marc McGovern's last minute skills saved this book from computer hell. I thank him too.

PARTHIAN   n e w   w r i t i n g

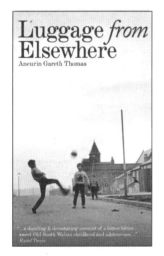

p a r t h i a n b o o k s . c o . u k